The Secret of the Ugly Brooch

by

Joy M Ross

Cover Art by *Tina Lynn Stout*

The Wild Rose Press, Inc.
PO Box 708
Adams Basin, NY 14410-0708
Visit us at www.thewildrosepress.com

Publishing History
First Edition, 2024
Trade Paperback ISBN 978-1-5092-5461-3
Digital ISBN 978-1-5092-5462-0

Published in the United States of America

Dedication

To my husband, who was my constant supporter, and gave honest critiques. I miss you.

My daughter and family, always excited when I would place in a contest. Son-in-law, I could not have made it this far without your geek skills. In your debt, I am.

A big thank you to Novel Idea, possibly the BEST critique group ever! (Yes, Renee, that is an exclamation point.)
Renee, Gene, Mary Ellen, Xaundra, Jim, Gerald, Vance, Nick, Yvonne, new Yvonne, Jill, Teresa and Jenny.

My Beta readers: Charlotte, Elaine and Kathie, already asking for my next book.

And certainly not least, Rhonda Penders of The Wild Rose Press for taking a chance on me. Melanie Billings, already so patient with me and my blunders.

A big thank you all for believing in me.

Chapter One

"I may have exactly what you want." Mr. Sun nodded and smiled, waved his finger toward the case at the back of the store, and turned in that direction. It was an old jewelry store with a jeweler to match. Emma had given into a sudden impulse to shop for her ten-year-old niece. She followed him.

"We have some nice birthstone pieces in now. Do you know if she likes silver, yellow gold, or white gold?"

"I think white gold." Emma hadn't thought that far ahead. Her gaze wandered over the glass cases. The displays were beautiful, and for a small store in the downtown area, she wondered how his business succeeded. She was the only customer in the store, and the sidewalks had few shoppers.

He stopped behind the counter, about midway between the other two cases. "Is her birthday in October or November?"

Emma hadn't given an exact date, and it was now well into October. "The thirtieth of this month. She was almost a Halloween baby." She eyed an attractive pair of tourmaline earrings inside the counter in white gold settings. They looked exactly like something Cassie would wear. From what she could see of the price tag, they might be affordable. That would be great if she could get a gift and avoid further shopping. It was best to buy now. Considering how she shopped, the more she looked, the more indecisive she became.

The old jeweler patted down his pockets as he looked inside the case. "Drat! Where are those keys?" He tried one more pocket and said, "I think I must have left the keys by the register. Just a minute, and I'll get them."

"That's fine. Take your time. I'll just look." Emma leaned against the counter and studied the contents as the jeweler shuffled toward the cash register. She shifted her weight to get a better look at another pair of earrings. Her cell phone, which teetered on the edge of its pocket, slipped and clattered to the floor.

Emma glanced down at the noise, then bent to retrieve the slender phone. As her hand was about to grab it, she heard the door's old-fashioned bell tinkle, and a rough male voice shouted, "Hold it! Hands up where I can see them!"

Emma froze, her hand stretched out for the cell phone. She turned to look toward the front of the store, where the jeweler had gone to get the keys. She could see the elderly man, hands raised in the air. He faced whoever was on the other side of the counter. She assumed that person had a gun, as the old man looked too frightened to move.

She couldn't stay in her crouched position for long as her legs might give out on her. For now, the center glass case and her bent position hid her from both the view of the man who'd entered the store and the jeweler. She looked around from her low position and assessed the situation. One of the cut-away entrances to get behind the counter was to her right, and if she stayed down, she might be able to slip behind it and remain out of sight. She figured if the robber had a gun, it was in her best interest that he remained ignorant of her presence.

She inched her way to the right to get behind the showcase. She could hear the old man pleading with the robber. "Take anything you want. I don't care. Don't hurt me."

"You have jewelry to repair? I need to see it."

Emma couldn't see the jeweler from her new position but heard him say, "It's all in the back."

"Then you and I are going to the back. Let's hurry— I don't have much time. Keep your hands where I can see them."

Footsteps sounded, and Emma had to move as she would be right where the robber could see her if he followed the old man to the back. She dropped to her hands and knees and reached the entrance between the cases as the robber passed by where she had been. She was in the passway between the showcases now, wishing she were smaller, or the cases were bigger. For now, this was the safest place to be, and she scrunched up as tiny as possible. Her heart pounded hard in her ears.

She looked up and saw round mirrors at each corner of the store and realized one of them could reflect her to the gunman if he bothered to look. She would also be able to see him. *Is that a good thing or a bad thing?* She also saw a couple of security cameras and breathed a brief sigh of relief.

I wonder if there's a panic button to signal the police. To find such a button would mean leaving her hiding place and the security it offered. She couldn't risk it.

She heard the gunman yell at the jeweler, and she hated her inability to do something. *Like what? Beat up the gunman myself? Hit him over the head? With what?* Her small purse was no weapon, and a jewelry store

3

didn't usually stock baseball bats.

She squeezed her legs up tighter while she debated what she could do. The robber yelled louder. He wanted something the old man had to repair. Emma understood bits and pieces of words. Things fell and crashed in the back room, and she believed the gunman pushed things around as he looked for something. The old man sounded more frightened by the second.

"Gimme that." It was the rough voice of the robber.

Things were silent for a moment. Then she heard the gunman again. "This is what I need."

There were sounds of a scuffle, more items fell and crashed. A single gunshot rang out.

Emma jerked at the sound of the gunfire. Her breath came in short gasps, and her heart beat frantically. She was afraid to look around the case and, at the sound of the gunman's quick footsteps, tightened her long legs and torso into the tiniest ball she could manage.

She faced the front of the store as the robber strode to exit. He paused before leaving. Straight brown hair fell over the collar of his sport coat, and he bore a slim build with broad shoulders. At her angle, she could only see his back and was afraid if she strained too much, she would make a sound that would alert him to her presence.

He slipped the gun under his jacket, and with the ease of the movement, Emma surmised he had a shoulder holster. He clasped his hand around something and quickly transferred it to his pocket. He moved so he faced one of the corner mirrors in the front of the store, and Emma had a brief but clear view of his face. He pulled a pair of sunglasses from his other pocket and slipped them on.

Emma ducked back before he glanced up and saw her. He seemed unconcerned about the security cameras recording his every move.

A dark, nondescript sedan pulled up to the curb in front of the store. The gunman stepped outside and slid into the front passenger seat. The car drove away from the curb, a terrified Emma still crouched below the counter.

****

When Emma was certain the car and the gunman were gone, she ran stooped over behind the counter to the workroom, where she'd heard the jeweler and the robber. She went into the curtained room, and by the work items lying about, it was evident it was the repair room. Drawers had been pulled open and dumped, and bits and pieces of jewelry were strewn about.

Then she saw the old jeweler.

He was splayed on the floor, bits of jewelry scattered all around. She had watched enough CSI and crime scene shows; she was certain he was dead. The gunman had shot him once in the forehead. He lay on his back, arms flung wide, legs crumpled under him. His eyes were open and glazed.

Emma started to approach, then thought better of it. There was nothing she could do for him now. She turned to go to the phone and call the police but stopped inside the curtain that separated the back room from the store.

Think a minute. What should I do? Should I call the police? What if they think I murdered the old man? Obviously, she didn't have a gun on her, but that might not stop them from arresting her. They could think she had hidden it somewhere.

No, calling the police is the right thing to do, and

the sooner, the better. She slipped out her cell phone and dialed 911. She hated that she could not think to call for help when the robber was screaming at the old jeweler, but she was terrified, and the thought never occurred to her.

When the operator answered, she stated, "I'm in Sun Jewelry. A man has been shot, and he's dead." She didn't know the exact address but was able to give the street name.

She looked down at the jeweler again. *He didn't deserve this! He seemed like a nice old man, just trying to make a living.*

She went to the front of the store, careful not to touch anything, and waited for the police. It seemed just seconds before she heard the scream of sirens approaching.

With that sound came a sense of urgency. She waited, although her senses screamed, "*Run, get out of here.*"

When the uniformed police stormed through the door, followed by the paramedics, she pointed toward the back of the store and stood silent, watching them go through the motions to secure the area and document everything they saw. One uniformed officer separated himself from the group and approached. She gave him her name and stated she had called 911.

"You were a witness?" he asked.

"I saw the man come into the store, heard him take the jeweler to the back, and heard the…gunshot." Shaking, she caught her breath and wrapped her arms around her middle. She didn't realize how shattering it would be to recall the last moments that had been so traumatic.

The officer was sympathetic. "Why don't you come outside, sit down, and catch your breath? We'll want to take your statement."

"Okay." Emma followed him outside to the ambulance. The technician hurried over.

"Witness needs a little bit of calming time, maybe a drink of water. The detective will want to talk to her." The officer hurried back to the jewelry store. Emma turned to the emergency tech, wondering what she should do.

"Just have a seat here, away from the excitement. Catch your breath." He handed her a cold bottle of water. "Are you hurt?"

"No. Just a little rattled. But I'm not hurt." Emma sipped the water and sat on the wide bumper of the vehicle while she waited. Not having been through anything like this before, she didn't know what to expect.

She smoothed her skirt and readjusted her position. A stray breeze blew a lock of dark hair across her face. Absently, she pushed it behind her ear. She watched the policemen work the scene and wasn't surprised when the coroner's wagon rolled up. There was no need for the ambulance to be there, although she was comforted by the emergency personnel around her.

She worked in a local attorney's office, a short distance from the jewelry store. It was a nice day that prompted a sudden desire to have a stroll and shop for her niece's upcoming birthday. The quiet little store looked inviting. What if she hadn't gone into the shop? Would the jeweler still have been killed? Yes, she was certain of that, the robber seemed intent on getting something from the old man. Her being there would not have prevented his fate.

My being there may yet serve a purpose. Maybe I can help catch the killer.

Her life had been on a treadmill for a while, and Emma had succumbed and let it be. But now, she needed to help the police catch the murderer.

After a deep breath, she smoothed her skirt, straightened her purse on her shoulder, made sure the troublesome cell phone was securely snuggled in its place, then looked around to find the officer who'd talked with her. He was talking to another man, who stared intently at her. Hands on hips, the man listened to the officer. He shifted his stance, and Emma saw the flash of a badge on his belt.

Detective. She wondered if he would be the one who would interview her. As if in answer to her thoughts, the man gave a final nod to the officer and walked toward her.

Emma watched his walk and made no pretense of not studying him. Dark hair curled above cobalt blue eyes, and he emanated sincerity and trust. *A good one for an interrogation, at least for the women. Unless his voice doesn't match his looks, he would be able to pry a confession out of a woman just on looks alone.*

He smiled an encouraging smile, and Emma responded. Then she hesitated. Mr. Sun still lay dead on the floor of his jewelry store. She dropped her smile and stood as the detective drew close. He stopped in front of her and pulled out a small notepad and pen from his inside pocket. He gave her his full attention. He was all business now.

There were no preliminaries. "I'm Detective Mike Wells, Tulsa PD. I understand you were a witness. Could I have your name, please?"

"Emma. Emma Stone." She gestured down the street. "I work nearby and just came into the store to shop."

They ran through what had happened, and the detective went over and over the circumstances. The more dogged he became, the less attractive Emma found him. When he said he would need her to come to the station to fill out a statement, she interrupted.

"I thought that was what I was doing." She looked at him, exasperated. She shook her head, then looked back up, eyes misting with tears.

"Look," she said, "I don't run into dead bodies every day. I don't hear people begging for their lives or even a gun being fired. It has been a bit much." She took a long, shaky breath. "Of course, I'll come to the station. I want to do everything I can to help. Just let me go to my work, and let them know, okay? It's just down the street."

"All right," he agreed. "Go tell your boss you need to be gone for the rest of the afternoon."

He watched as she gathered her purse and sweater and hurried off to the law firm. A reporter came up and caught his attention. When he looked back, ten minutes had passed. Where was his witness?

Chapter Two

"So did you get it?" Al drove through the streets of downtown Tulsa, no small feat at midday. He glanced nervously behind him. Any minute, several police cars ablaze with lights and sirens could descend on them.

"Yeah, I got it." Joseph tightened his seat belt, and he noticed Al was pushing the speed limit. They had already discussed the need to stay within the limit to avoid drawing attention. Al was a good driver, and Joseph forced himself to relax. They had practiced this run until they were both tired of it, and everything should go smoothly.

"I shot the jeweler."

"What?" Al cursed under his breath. "Why'd you do that? Couldn't you just get the stupid brooch thing and get out of there? No one was supposed to get hurt. Did you kill him?"

"Yes." Joseph sighed and kicked back in the seat. He put his arm up on the door and rested his head on his hand. "When he finally showed me the brooch, I reached for it, and at the same time, he pushed me and reached for the gun. It was a reflex; the gun went off." He took off his sunglasses and rubbed his eyes. Putting them back on, he said, "I'm just glad you were outside on time to pick me back up. No delays, that's good."

"What about the girl? Was she still in the store?"

"What girl?" Joseph didn't remember a girl.

"How could you forget? The one who went in right before you killed the video feed. We both saw her—a real babe, long legs, short skirt. We figured she could distract the old man long enough for you to take care of the video." Al looked across at his partner, a worried scowl on his face. "Maybe she was in and out. Ya think?"

There was a bad sinking feeling in the pit of Joseph's stomach. He had been so caught up in the robbery, dealing with the old jeweler. Then things went sideways, and the girl completely slipped his mind. It was careless and unlike him to let a detail like a possible witness get past him.

He struggled to remember the store interior. The old jeweler was by the register. Mentally, he played back the rest of the store as he scanned it. He didn't see anyone else. *What was the old man doing? Was he talking to anyone? No*. He convinced himself the girl *must* have left the store. But a niggling doubt prevailed, and he didn't like it. He liked to deal with certainties, no loose ends. If he absolutely had to, he would eliminate this one.

A fine mess I've gotten into. I really should retire; my reflexes aren't what they used to be. I didn't anticipate the old guy making a stupid move like that.

Joseph Malone was not a killer, had never killed anyone in his entire career. He'd been convinced to take this job, an easy one, he was told. Then, he could retire and live comfortably amongst his collection of fine art and hefty bank accounts. He had his disappearance all planned out, and now that would have to wait.

Joseph was being paid a lot of money for this job, and his professionalism was at stake. His clients got their money's worth. He would have to do whatever had to be done to make this right. His paying clients deserved that.

"Slight change of plans, Al. Head over to the parking garage. I'm gonna get my car and go back. I have to make sure there were no witnesses."

Al looked at him. "Man, you gotta be kiddin'. Go back into that? What about our plans? What am I supposed to do? I have a stake in this, too."

Joseph shook his head and glanced at his partner. "When have I ever let you down? Drop me off and go on to the apartment as planned. Stay off the turnpike. I'll meet you there as soon as I can. If I run into a problem, I'll call you."

"Okay," Al grumbled as he made a right turn to go east on Second. He pulled into an ancient parking garage that had neither security cameras nor guards. It had been one of Joseph's favorite places to park his car, an old 2000 brown sedan. It ran great but looked like it had seen better days. Because of that, Joseph claimed people looked right over it.

Al stopped behind the old car, and his passenger stepped out. He was counting on a second look from a tall, dark-haired beauty to confirm if he did or did not have a witness to his crime. He couldn't let the brooch out of his sight. He checked the inside pocket of his jacket, making sure it was secure.

Checking his watch, he walked to the driver's door of the car and addressed Al. "It's one thirty now. I'll call you tonight at eight."

Al shifted the car into drive. "Okay. I'll be waiting." The car moved forward, and Joseph walked to the old car.

Backing out of his space, he drove slowly, careful to keep in the flow of traffic. He knew he wouldn't be able to get near the jewelry store for the police and onlookers, and he really didn't want to get too close, either.

The *babe,* as Al had described her—and Joseph vaguely remembered her—had long dark hair and wore a black skirt that stopped above her knees. Long shapely legs, slim figure. If he did get close enough to the store and saw such a girl talking to a detective, he would get out of there as soon as possible before she had a chance to see him. He imagined the girl, a flash of recognition on her face as she pointed and shouted, "That's him!" while the police gave chase. Not a good scenario.

Careful to keep in the flow of traffic, he drove slowly. He had no idea where the girl had come from, or if she had left the store, where she might be going. Her clothes were business wear, so perhaps she worked at one of the local attorney's offices—there were many in this part of town. He headed toward the jewelry store, his eye on the pedestrian traffic.

A short distance from the store, Joseph kept his head down as he drove. He slipped by the shop, past all the police and ambulance. He scanned the crowd but didn't see the girl among the onlookers or the officers. He breathed a sigh of relief. At least so far, maybe she hadn't talked to the police, and even better, maybe she didn't even exist as a witness.

That sinking feeling hit him in the stomach again as he reached the next street. Ahead of him and to his left, a tall, dark-haired girl walked briskly along the sidewalk. Was it his imagination, or was there a nervousness to her walk? She had her head down as though she wanted to get to her destination as quickly as possible.

He studied her in his rearview mirror as he passed. She glanced up at him, but there was no recognition on her face. However, at that angle, she couldn't see his face clearly. He would try to stay out of her line of sight but watch where she was going. He continued down the street and parallel parked on the other side, a little ahead. From this vantage point, he could watch her as she approached and went past him. He turned off the engine and waited.

****

Emma made a quick stop at the office and told them she would be gone the rest of the day. Of course, they had questions. They'd heard the sirens. She explained it was important and was a request by the Tulsa police, showing them the detective's card. She knew not to say she was a witness to a murder. It would only open more questions. She hurried out, intent on getting back to the police. She glanced around, seeing other pedestrians and traffic on the street.

She was on a one-way street, and all the traffic flowed forward past her. One car in particular, an older four-door sedan, traveled a little slower than the others, and it pulled over and parked ahead. It drew her attention. When she saw the tall, broad-shouldered man get out of the car and turn toward her, the blood drained from her face. Emma spun around and started back the direction she came.

The detective who said he would watch her had turned away and was talking to someone who had a microphone in his face. She glanced over her shoulder to see if the man followed her. He waited for traffic to clear, then crossed the street behind her. She gasped and ran faster, then fled around the corner.

Emma appraised her situation. The killer was between her and the police. He would get to her before she could get their attention. *Drat that detective, Mike*

Wells, getting distracted by a reporter. I'm going to give him an earful next time I see him.

Looking around to see where she could escape, there was the street and parking lot to cross if she wanted to continue down the street or closer, a funeral home. She chose the funeral home. Emma hurried down the sidewalk, jerked open the door, and stepped inside. She hoped the killer had not seen her come this way. She headed for the ladies' restroom. A somber middle-aged man in a dark suit stepped from a side parlor, where she assumed a funeral was about to be held. There were no other patrons in the lobby.

"Good afternoon," he greeted her. "Are you here for Mr. Kerwood's service?"

Without thinking, she blurted, "Yes, yes. I, uh, just need to freshen up." Emma hoped she didn't sound like an idiot. She had no intention of attending a funeral, only wanted to hide out in the restroom long enough to lose the man who followed her.

"Right this way." He stepped in front of her, and pointed to the ladies' room that was in plain sight. "The service will begin in a few minutes. Please be sure to sign in when you enter." Then he turned and walked back toward the other room.

Emma hurried to the restroom. Shutting the door, she heaved a big sigh. However, she didn't know if she had gained anything. *Did the killer see me come in? If so, would he follow me inside or wait outside?* She glanced in the mirror, her cheeks flushed from the exertion and excitement, her hair slightly disheveled, and her sweater hanging off her arm.

She would do what she could to alter her appearance and clean up. In her purse, she found a clasp and a couple of barrettes. Emma swept her hair up and worked it into a high bun, using the barrettes to curtail any loose strands at the side of her head. Then she reached into her purse again and produced the pair of black plastic-rimmed glasses she wore while reading. They were not very complimentary; she thought they made her appear scholarly.

A bit of powder on her cheeks to tone down the blush, a bit of lip gloss, and that was all she could do for her face and hair. She couldn't change her clothing, but she could take off the sweater. If he saw her in the pews, he would see a woman with her hair up in a white blouse, instead of a black sweater.

She checked the time. It had only been five minutes. She placed her ear to the crack in the door. There were only soft strains of a hymn, no doubt a program designed to comfort mourners. She eased the door open a notch; still heard nothing but the hymn, no voices. She shifted her weight and adjusted her purse, snuggled the troublesome cell phone back into its pocket, and eased the door open just a bit more. She saw no one. The entrance was completely blocked from her line of sight. She was ready to give up and consider her next move when the funeral director came into view. He stood outside the parlor, hands clasped in front, prepared to patiently wait all day for family mourners.

Emma cursed silently. She could wait longer, and the funeral director would begin to wonder what was keeping her, or she could step out and take a seat and thus try to wait out her pursuer.

She decided to take her chances and stepped out of the restroom toward the funeral director.

"I am so sorry for your loss," he spoke in a low tone

and, with an outstretched arm, indicated the parlor she should enter. "Are you family?"

There were pews on both sides of the room, and the parlor itself was relatively small. Off to the side and at the front, closest to the casket, was a special area set aside, she assumed, for the family. Some of the seats were obscured by a large screen for privacy from the rest of the mourners. She needed to be seated there.

"Yes," she answered to his question. The funeral director, Brad Thomas, by his elegant name badge, led her to the family section and indicated a seat at the front of the private pews.

"I think I'll sit here if that's all right." She moved to the back of the pews before he could object. "There are other family members who were closer to, uh, him than me." She tried to cover up her faux pas as she smiled and took a seat. She realized she didn't even know the name of the man whose funeral she was attending other than Mr. Kerwood. But Brad Thomas didn't need to know that.

"As you wish." He didn't seem at all concerned about her manner and headed to the front of the parlor to wait for other mourners.

Emma exhaled. She was behind a screen, hidden from anyone who would walk in. Surely, if the man pursuing her tried to take her by force, the funeral director would call the police. Thinking of the police, she mentally groaned. *Why didn't I call the police the minute I stepped inside the funeral home? How stupid was that?*

Emma grabbed her purse to extract her cell phone and call Detective Wells. Just as she touched it, another patron entered the private section and looked directly at her. He smiled and nodded to her, then sat in the front row.

What was that about? Emma wondered. She left her phone alone. *I'll call Detective Wells the minute this is over.* She studied the back of the man who had eyed her so pointedly. Older, distinguished, tall with snow-white hair. Not her pursuer in disguise.

Idly, she opened the little pamphlet Mr. Thomas had handed her detailing the life of Mr. Kerwood. *So sad.* They can take his whole life and condense it into this little booklet.

Reading, she learned he was Jonathan Louis Kerwood, born in Waynesville, Missouri. He was ninety-two years old when he died. He lived a good, long life.

He had been married, his wife preceding him in death seven years earlier. No children. Parents, siblings, deceased. He worked for an insurance and annuity firm most of his life. There was no church affiliation noted, which she thought a little unusual.

She closed the booklet and looked around. There was the casket with Mr. Kerwood resting in it, she presumed. She hadn't glanced at him as she had tried to hurry discreetly to a seat. The pulpit for the preacher stood beyond that. A big spray of flowers sat on the casket, but no others. *Interesting. Mr. Kerwood mustn't have been extremely popular.* Except for the white-haired man, she hadn't heard or seen any other mourners shuffle in.

The preacher came out of a side door behind the pulpit, placed his bible on the pedestal, and looked out at the mourners. Or rather, where the mourners should have been. He contained his surprise at seeing only two.

The service began. Brad Thomas sat in the front

pew, along with one other young man dressed in a similar dark suit. A hidden organist played the strains of "Amazing Grace."

After the song died away, the preacher read his eulogy for Jonathan Kerwood, giving basically the same information in verbal form as the booklet. Jonathan had been an only child, and there were no members of the Kerwood family left. That would help explain the lack of mourners. She guessed he must not have had any friends or neighbors either.

This is really bizarre. Emma waited as the preacher wound down his sermon. She glanced at her watch. It had been a short service, barely fifteen minutes. The organist played another hymn while the four of them sat in contemplative, respectful silence.

Mr. Thomas came and made a slight inclination with his hand that it was time to rise and view Mr. Kerwood one final time.

Mr. White Hair rose, and so did Emma. White Hair took a quick look and then moved on down the aisle before Emma was past the front row. *How rude.* He walked down the aisle to the parlor entrance and left before Emma arrived at the casket. She walked forward, not sure what to do next.

View the body. Yes, that needs to be done. Then, walk to the door of the parlor, where White Hair went. Then what? Would the killer be waiting for her? Had Emma helped her situation at all with this scheme to try to hide from the killer?

As she approached Mr. Thomas, he leaned toward her. In a low voice, he said there was a family limousine at her disposal to carry her to the burial site if she wished to attend. Without thinking, Emma whispered, "Yes.

Where is it?" When he said it was in the back, behind the hearse, she nodded.

Why did I do that? She was getting in deeper, and she needed to call the police. She felt safe around Mr. Thomas and his funeral staff, and the urgency to flee was less.

Now at the casket, she gazed silently at the old man within. *He looks pretty good for ninety-two.* Typical of his age group, he didn't seem to have excess flesh, and his suit looked expensive. Mr. Kerwood was not a large man, had very little hair left, and his ears and nose seemed disproportionately large for his head. She recalled the comments uttered sincerely by family at funerals she attended. *He looked really nice,* came to mind, and fit Mr. Kerwood.

She stood for a respectful time, turned, and walked to the front lobby. There were no sad-eyed people standing around to console her or comfort her with words of how sorry they were for her loss.

The young man who sat beside Brad Thomas asked her if she would be riding in the family limo. When she nodded, he led her to a parking area where the hearse and limo waited. Emma glanced about, but the parking lot was bordered on three sides by other buildings. No killer skulked in the shadows. Brad Thomas's young helper opened the door. She slid in and plopped down comfortably on the plush seat. As he shut the door, she reached and flipped the lock.

Now, call the police. She reached for her phone as Mr. Kerwood's casket was placed in the hearse.

Mr. Thomas slid into the driver's seat of the hearse, and his young employee approached Emma's limousine. Sensing his intent to drive, she flipped the door switch so he could gain entry. Emma replaced the phone. This was not the time. She leaned back in her seat and closed her eyes.

The passenger door opened, and Emma jumped and squealed in surprise. It was Mr. White Hair. He looked at her, eyebrows raised.

"I'm sorry if I startled you, my dear." His voice was polite and refined. One brief sentence, and Emma got the impression he spoke his words carefully and with thought.

"Oh, that's okay. I'm just a little jittery, that's all. Funerals are very emotional, you know." Emma made light of it and smiled as she adjusted her skirt.

Mr. White Hair sat on the plush seat opposite her. He studied her for a second before he leaned forward, stretching out his hand. "Paul Johnson," he said. "And you are?"

"Emma Stone." She shook his hand. "Pleased to meet you. Albeit not under the best of circumstances."

"I agree." He settled back and crossed his legs. That's when Emma noticed the briefcase on the seat beside him. *Who takes a briefcase to a funeral?*

He spoke again. "You sat in the family section. Are you related to Mr. Kerwood?"

"More of a friend."

The hearse moved, followed by the limo. Emma tried to look out the windows without appearing to be anxious. She really could have done without Mr. Johnson's company. She was counting on the tinted windows and privacy so she could study the streets as they left the parking lot to make sure the killer wasn't loitering around. With Mr. Johnson sitting across from her, watching her, she didn't want him to think she was, well, weird.

They exited the parking lot, continuing down the street at a slow roll. So far, she had not seen any sign of the killer. Emma had been holding her breath without realizing it. She let it out and relaxed. She looked out the window beside her, schooling her expression (she hoped) as someone studying the landscape. *Look bored.*

"How did you know Mr. Kerwood?"

Emma looked at Mr. Johnson. *I really wish he would just leave it alone.* She didn't want to admit that she ducked into Mr. Kerwood's funeral to escape someone who probably wanted to kill her. However, Johnson's expression was only curious. No criticism showed on his features.

Rather than answering, she pointedly looked at his briefcase. "How did *you* know him?" she countered.

"He was my client. I'm an attorney."

"Oh." *That explains the briefcase. Sort of. Maybe there were some last-minute items to finalize with the funeral home.*

She looked out the window again, hoping Mr. Johnson would forget he had asked twice what her relationship was with Mr. Kerwood. Emma needed time to think up a reasonable story. Lying was not something she did well.

Mr. Johnson didn't ask her again. They'd left the downtown area, traveling on the highway leading east out of town. She assumed they were going to Floral Haven Memorial Park, situated between Tulsa and Broken Arrow.

When they had passed all the exits that led to Floral Haven, she felt a wave of panic and looked directly at Mr. Johnson. "Where are we going?" she asked, suddenly anxious.

"Grove," Mr. Johnson answered. He looked at her, a question in his eyes. "Surely you knew Mr. Kerwood lived in Grove."

"Oh, yes, yes, of course, I forgot. My thoughts are not so clear today." She mumbled her apology, remembering that fact had been mentioned in his memorial booklet. She sat back to watch the city and the countryside roll by. It was going to be a long ride, just her and Mr. Johnson.

Chapter Three

The girl made a quick right and ducked out of Joseph's sight. He moved quickly away from the car and ignored the parking meter, his attention focused on her. A few cars away, a policeman put a ticket under the windshield wiper of a parked car.

Half-walking, half-jogging, Joseph headed in the direction Emma disappeared. He didn't know what spooked her, but that wasn't his concern now. He needed to find her and get her taken care of quietly. Joseph cursed himself for being so careless as to allow a possible witness to escape.

Waiting for a couple of cars to pass, Joseph crossed the avenue and entered the small street where the girl had darted. There were several possibilities in front of him where she could have gone, none of them a sure thing. A large parking garage loomed to his left, three stories tall and relatively dark in broad daylight, a pawn shop where the proprietor might be willing to help a frightened young woman, a couple of attorney offices, and a funeral home. Suddenly, his desire to follow didn't seem like such a good idea—there were too many sources of help for her and definite problems for him.

Joseph turned back and ran across the street to his car, keeping his eye out should the girl reappear. In his head, he could hear her shouting, *That's HIM!* a whole crowd of policemen behind her, ready to chase him.

He unlocked his car and slid behind the wheel. That's when he noticed the bright pink ticket under his wiper. He stepped out and reached around to snatch it. *A parking ticket?* He threw it aside, cursing under his breath. Darned if his day didn't get better and better.

****

Detective Wells frowned and looked in the direction Emma had gone. He turned to his partner, Jim, advised him where he was going, and headed down the street. Emma had not given him the name of the law firm where she worked. Neither he nor the other officer had gotten a cell number for her either, an oversight he would have to explain. He went into a couple of offices, but they were not the correct businesses.

He didn't have time to track her down. She had given him a short version of what happened, and he would catch up with her later. Emma would have some explaining to do when he did. Mike heaved a big sigh, shoving his hand in his pocket. His left hand lifted and ran through his short dark hair, a nervous habit when things weren't going smoothly. He turned his thoughts to the Sun family.

The jeweler, Mr. Sun, was a respected member of the community. His family had been in the Tulsa area for four generations, and he or a family member always had operated this little jewelry store. He was known for detailed work, both in designing and repairing jewelry, and his work was of the highest quality.

There wasn't a lot more he could do here. He had to break the news to Mrs. Sun. He would do that now and then go to the station and see the surveillance tape.

****

The scene with Mrs. Sun was as bad as he had

25

imagined. Mr. and Mrs. Sun had been married for over forty-five years and were devoted to each other and their family. They raised three daughters and a son, but only one daughter had shown any interest in continuing the jewelry business. That daughter was home at the time he arrived, so Mrs. Sun was not alone when he delivered the bad news. He left them sobbing in each other's arms, knowing what a difficult and sorrowful time they had ahead of them. He distanced himself from his emotions. It was a two-edged sword. He didn't want to appear to be a cold-hearted bastard, but on the other hand, if he let his emotions rule, he wouldn't be very good at his job.

Leaving the modest neighborhood behind, he trained his thoughts on the case at hand. He headed to the station, hoping there might be something on surveillance video or that Emma had reappeared.

He received a call as he was parking outside the police building. It was his partner, Jim. "Are you on your way back? The video is here…" He paused. "Where is the witness anyway?"

Jim was excited, his speech quick and scattered. His partner had recently been made detective, and this was his first case. "I'm right outside," Mike answered. "Give me about five minutes. And I don't know where Emma is."

He hurried into the building and took the elevator to the third floor. He entered the detective division, and long strides took him back to where the captain, Jim, and other officers waited. He was surprised the captain had made Jim contain his enthusiasm and wait. Sometimes the captain seemed to want to remind them who really was in charge. For whatever reason, Mike was glad he made them wait. He wanted to see the tape for the first time along with the others.

Jim was sitting on the edge of his chair, jiggling his leg in nervousness. Mike knew they would see this tape several times before the case was closed, but the first viewing was usually the most exciting, especially if there was any information to be gathered from it. He placed his hand on Jim's shoulder, and his partner almost leaped out of the chair.

"Sorry, guy, didn't mean to startle you." Mike looked around at the other men. "If you've been waiting on me, I'm just as anxious as you to see this."

The captain picked up the video and slid it into the old VCR player. "There was only one camera in the corner of the store, and it was set up to swivel from one side of the store to the other. Going from the front door to the side and back again. Old system." He punched a button to make the video play. They all grew silent, gazes locked on the monitor.

The screen came alive and displayed an empty gray view of the interior of the small jewelry store. No one there. They watched as the video camera did a painstakingly slow crawl from the door to the side of the store, catching all the jewelry cases and where customers would be standing.

The camera is fairly accurate. If someone were trying to pocket something and the camera happened to be on them, it would certainly catch them. Mike kept his gaze on the screen. The camera moved to the extreme right. Movement to the left showed someone had come in. They all leaned sideways to help the camera move back to the left so that they could see who entered. It slowly showed the backside, then the right side, and finally, the frontal view of a slender young woman. She spoke to someone behind the counter, assumingly Mr. Sun.

Finally, it showed both the young woman and Mr. Sun. She gazed down into the showcase and pointed to something. Mr. Sun nodded and gestured also; his left hand indicated the young woman might find something over to her right. It was at this point that the young woman turned and looked in the direction that he had gestured. It was clearly Emma.

Mr. Sun and Emma moved to the right where he'd indicated, out of the camera's sight again. Inch by inch, the camera moved over to the direction they had gone and caught Mr. Sun returning to the left, the young woman remaining out of camera range. It appeared he might be heading to the cash register. The tape blinked and went to snow.

Apparently, that was where the feed line had been cut.

The men in the room visibly relaxed and groaned. Mike hadn't realized how tense he had become. He knew the shooting wouldn't be on it, or else why cut the line? But yet unaware of what they would see. He looked around at the small group.

"Well," he said. "It's up to me to find our witness. Again."

****

Emma sat quietly throughout the graveside service; Mr. Paul Johnson sat one chair away. Mr. Thomas stood to the side. The preacher had intoned another brief service and committed Mr. Kerwood's body to the earth. Mr. Thomas handed her a single white rose from the arrangement covering the casket, and she took it gently. All the time during the brief service, Emma wondered how on earth she would survive the ride back to Tulsa with Mr. Johnson. He hadn't talked further on the trip to the burial, but she wondered how much longer he could keep his silence. Emma could just *feel* his curiosity.

The preacher intoned a brief prayer, and the service was over. Emma started back to the limousine. Mr. Thomas was there ahead of her and stood waiting, holding her door open. He addressed her. "I just need a few words with the burial crew and Mr. Johnson. I'll be right back to take you to the funeral home."

"Thank you," she murmured, climbing in. The interior of the limo was cool. Mr. Thomas had thoughtfully started the engine early, and the air conditioner kept the interior comfortable. He shut the door behind her. Considering his last statement, she surmised Mr. Johnson might not be riding back with her.

Mr. Thomas left the limo and returned to the grave site. Emma felt immediately more relaxed. Another dark sedan pulled up before the service was over, remaining at a distance. A driver emerged from it, only to stand waiting. Perhaps, she thought, it was Mr. Johnson's ride back to the office. Since Mr. Kerwood had a home in Grove, perhaps Mr. Johnson's office was in Grove.

A pretty town, Emma had noted as they rode through Grove to the cemetery. Especially the lake—she loved the lake. Large and winding, the water a deep blue, with trees right up to the shoreline. There had been a light breeze, evidenced by the slight movement of the leaves on the trees and slight rippling of the lake water, and several sailboats were in full sail. As they crossed one of the bridges that passed over the lake, Emma envied the people on the sailboats, wishing she were out there, soaking up the sun and the lake breeze. She might even doze a little bit, while someone else would be monitoring the sails and making sure they didn't crash into something.

Ah, that would be a nice life. Emma returned to reality as Mr. Thomas re-entered the driver's seat. He pushed the intercom button. "Miss Stone?"

Emma leaned forward, eyebrows raised. "Yes?"

"Did you sign in as a guest for the service?"

Emma thought. No, in such a hurry to be seated and out of sight, she hadn't even considered it. "No, I didn't."

"You need to do that when we get back. It's very important. I'll remind you again when we arrive."

"All right." Emma sighed and leaned back as Mr. Thomas eased the limo down the tiny road in the cemetery and onto the paved county road. *Why was it so important to sign the register? After all, Mr. Kerwood seems wealthy enough. Surely, they aren't going to stick me for his expenses just because I was the only one who showed up.*

Emma was curious about the deceased. Had he been a horrible man, and no one liked him? Was that why no one came to his funeral? Or was he just a shy, quiet hermit? Evidently, from the tiny brochure, there wasn't any family, or they were so far distanced that he hadn't kept in touch with them.

Mr. Kerwood had a home in Grove. Emma wondered what it was like. She allowed a daydream, and in her thoughts, she wandered through a stately mansion. Having risen from a good night's sleep, wrapped in a warm fluffy robe, the aroma of fresh hot coffee wafted up to her from the cup in her grasp. Or maybe it was evening, time for a quiet dinner. Or better yet, a dinner *party* with her closest friends. Perhaps they would be out on the veranda that overlooked the lake, and her butler would announce dinner was served. They would all go in for an elegant meal prepared by a five-star chef. Ah, that would be the life. Emma sighed. It wasn't her reality.

Her mind took a more depressing turn. Was Mr. Kerwood's home a tiny, run-down shack? But no, that didn't seem to fit her perception of the deceased. She obviously didn't know him but somehow sensed he was not poor.

Emma set her daydreams aside and remembered, *call the detective.* She retrieved her phone and punched it open. Dead. She looked around, hoping to see a charging station. While the limo was nice, it wasn't *that* nice. Emma sighed and leaned back. As soon as she was in her own car, the worrisome device would be plugged in, and she'd call Detective Wells. Surely, the killer was no longer lingering. Emma hoped that he didn't know where she'd gone, but not knowing was a question she was going to have to deal with until she knew for sure.

In the comfort of the vehicle and feeling safe, Emma dozed. She woke with a start when they arrived at the funeral home.

Emma followed Mr. Thomas into the building. She glanced about, hoping she would not see the killer. If she did, she would call the police immediately from the business. The parking lot was small and wedged between the funeral home and other businesses, so there was not a lot of observing she could do. The killer could be in the parking garage across the street, with a high-power rifle aimed at her back.

Emma was very relieved when they stepped inside the quiet confines of the funeral parlor.

****

The guest register book had been cleared, so Mr. Thomas took a few moments to find it. He requested Emma wait in his office, which was fine with her as it was even more isolated. While she waited, she chafed at being so paranoid. She mentally argued whether paranoia was keeping her alive or driving her crazy when he returned with the book.

He laid the book on the desk in front of her, open to the first page. No other names were on it. "If you would just sign on one of these lines, Miss Stone, and please include your address."

Emma signed her name, her handwriting neat and legible. "Why do you want my address? I've never given my address before in a guest book."

"Mr. Johnson requested it for his firm."

Emma looked at Mr. Thomas, puzzled. A quick decision made, she scribbled down her parents' address, where she still had the occasional piece of mail delivered. What harm could it do? They were a long-established funeral home; Mr. Johnson was probably from a reputable law firm. Somehow, she did not think Mr. Thomas or Mr. Johnson were either going to make illegal use of her address. She asked, "What will you do with my address and this book?"

Mr. Thomas closed the book and put it on the corner of his desk. "Your address will not go further than this book, and the book goes to Mr. Johnson. It will be mailed to his firm in the morning."

"Ah, good." She was relieved to hear that. Now that Emma had no further reason to linger at the funeral home, she stood and shook Mr. Thomas's hand.

"It was a very good service." Emma hesitated. She should have been able to come up with something better than that. However, Mr. Thomas didn't seem offended. He merely smiled as though he understood and escorted her to the door.

Realizing she still had to walk to her car to get home, Emma asked if she could call a cab and if he would mind if she waited inside.

"Of course not, but if you need a ride, we'll be glad to provide it." He turned his head to the side as he thought, "But it won't be in the limo. Just a sedan."

"Oh, that would be great! I would be ever so grateful, and I don't need to go far." Emma couldn't believe her good luck. Mr. Thomas went to arrange her ride and invited her to have a seat in the lobby while he went to get the car.

Emma sat, happy to wait. Mr. Thomas and his funeral home were certainly going out of their way to be kind. She thought it was a little strange, but then again, she had never been to a funeral where only one person was in attendance.

****

His grandson was located and instructed him to drive Miss Emma to another location and bring the sedan back around to the exit door. He had been firmly instructed by Paul Johnson that, number one, he was to get Miss Emma's full name and address and, number two, provide any request that she asked in relation to the funeral. Since she needed a ride somewhere, that fell within the realm of those instructions.

He returned to Emma and showed her to the waiting sedan. His grandson, Brandon, would be glad to drive her wherever she needed. Emma shook Mr. Thomas's hand again, thanking him sincerely for all he had done for her.

Once in the car, which thankfully was deeply tinted, Brandon asked where Emma needed to go. She gave the address of the parking garage where her car was parked. When they arrived, Emma looked around.

"Are you looking for someone?" Brandon asked.

"No. Yes. Maybe." Emma sighed as she continued to look around nervously. "Do you see anyone that seems to be, like, lurking?"

Brandon looked around, too. The parking garage was half full. Apparently, some workers had taken an afternoon off. He didn't see anyone and said so. Then added, "I'll get your door, and I can see better."

He exited and opened her door for her to depart. Emma was shamefaced. *He must think I am an idiot.* Emma hurried to her red compact sedan. She pressed the lock release as she walked toward it.

Brandon returned to the sedan and waited for Emma's car to start.

Emma sat in the car briefly before starting it. Suppose the killer had found her car and installed a bomb that would explode when the car started? She shook her head to clear it. That was not something that happened in the real world and to her. It was only on TV. She started the car, backed out of the parking space, and followed Brandon out of the parking garage. He turned to go to the funeral home and Emma to her apartment. No one followed her.

Chapter Four

Friday morning dawned a clear autumn day. Emma was a nervous wreck and considered calling in sick. Things at work had indicated it would be a quiet day. And it was Friday.

Perched on a stool at her kitchen counter, a cup of coffee steamed before her. She had ladled in more than her usual amount of cream and sipped it tentatively. Up most of the night, she still had not called the police, and she had to do that. *Talk to that detective, Mike Something.* She hoped he had enough information. Maybe he didn't need to talk to her anymore. What Emma was terrified of was the killer. She didn't want him to find her. If she went to the police, would he discover her identity, and could the police protect her? In the movies, they always said they could, but then two out of three witnesses wound up dead.

A couple of friends called, but Emma begged off going out, telling them she had an upset stomach. Her mom called, too, one of her random calls to check on her daughter. It took all she could muster not to cry and let it all out to her mother, but she stuck to her upset stomach story and said she would call back when she felt better.

Her insides churned. She wanted to confide in someone but was afraid in doing so, she would not feel any better and possibly get a confidant in deep water with her.

A light tap on her leg, and she looked down. A large, orange-striped cat stood on his hind legs, begging for attention. He looked her in the eyes and meowed pitifully. Once he was scratched behind the ears, he lowered all legs to the floor, walked over to his food bowl, and sat down. He looked at her, looked at his empty food dish again, then back at her. He let out another plaintive meow as she slid off the stool.

"Okay, okay, I'll get your breakfast." Emma pulled his bag of food from under the counter and dipped some out, which he attacked. "You'd think you were starving and never fed." She said affectionately and rubbed the big orange marmalade cat on the head.

He paused long enough to rub back against her hand, then dived back to his food. Marms had been her one source of comfort during the night, cuddled up next to her on the couch, in the bed, or back on the couch. Wherever she managed to land while she worried about the consequences of Thursday's events. She finally had a few hours of restless sleep, and when she woke, he still slept beside her. Her hours of tossing and turning had not disturbed him.

She returned to her coffee, slipping a couple of pieces of wheat bread into the toaster. She needed some sustenance. She only had a chocolate milkshake for dinner, and it hadn't lasted until this morning. Munching on the toast, she decided she would go to work as normal and get through the day as best she could. Surely, the killer was long gone by now. Maybe by the end of the day, she could decide what to do. She headed for the shower, determined to try to make this day as normal as possible. One thing she did know: her conscience would not let her carry on this way, even if she was in danger.

Something had to be done.

****

Joseph Malone had also spent a restless night. The scene with the jeweler occasionally crept into his consciousness. He shoved it back in the far corners of his mind, then turned over and tried to return to sleep. Not a warm and fuzzy person, the coldness of his personality helped shape him into the professional criminal he was. Everyone who knew him knew he stole things. Expensive things, rare things. But he didn't kill people.

Today was an important day. He had an appointment with the man he identified as the Buyer, and Joseph would receive his payment. That would be the end of their relationship, and they would each go their separate ways. The brooch would go into the hands of the Buyer, and Joseph could walk away to retirement.

He finished his shower, dried, and threw on a robe. He stepped out to check on Al, see what he was doing. He hoped he had made breakfast.

Al must have read his mind, as the tiny kitchen table was set with two cups of coffee, two paper plates, and plastic ware. Waffles, fresh from the toaster, syrup, and sausages, waited for him. Besides toasted waffles, Joseph smelled a light scent of cigarettes. Al stood by the balcony doors, his hands waving as he tried to dispel the evidence. He grinned at Joseph.

A small TV played the morning local news. Joseph nodded toward it. "They say anything about the robbery?"

"Pretty much the same thing as the paper. They haven't determined why he was shot; said nothing seemed to be taken."

"Did they mention a witness?" He had briefed Al on

his unsuccessful attempt to follow the girl. If the newspaper and TV didn't mention her, there was still a chance she didn't exist.

"No. They don't have any leads. And maybe that girl really isn't a witness. Maybe you just scared her, and she ran. You know how many creeps go after young women these days."

"Creeps? So, she may see me and think a maniac is after her?"

"You know what I mean."

"I think she saw me and recognized me."

"Then maybe she'll stay in hiding, afraid to get involved. There's a lot of that these days, too."

"Thanks for the breakfast," Joseph said as he sat. "My appointment with the Buyer is pretty early." He cut into the waffle and looked at his partner. "I assume you'll head out right away."

"Yeh. As soon as you pay me, I'm gone." Now that the job was completed, Al was ready to disappear. They worked together occasionally, Al usually providing the getaway vehicle. This case, unexpectedly involving murder, made him anxious to move on.

They finished their breakfast in silence. Al picked up his dishes and placed them in the trash. A question niggled at him.

"Why did you shoot him? You usually don't even carry a gun."

Joseph frowned as he answered. "It was the Buyer's idea. He wanted to make sure I could convince the jeweler to give up the brooch. After he handed it to me, as I was putting it in my pocket, the old man leaped on me. He was so frail; I didn't expect that. It caught me off guard. The gun went off." He took another sip. "I wish I had never taken this job."

Al had no response. He waited, unsure what to say or do next.

Joseph stood and told him, "Just a minute. I'll get your pay, and you can leave."

"Okay."

Joseph retrieved the envelope that held Al's pay from the bedroom. When he returned, Al waited at the apartment door. He had already gathered up his backpack and his personal items.

"Here." Joseph handed him the envelope. "There's a little extra in there. I always appreciate what a good job you do."

Al opened the door to exit and gave his partner a quick handshake. "Have a good rest of your life."

Joseph shut the door after him.

****

In about an hour, he would meet with the man he referred to as the Buyer. In a coffee house/internet bar, the brooch would be traded for payment. Exchanges like this Joseph preferred in an open, public area, as there was less likelihood the Buyer would pay him in another way other than monetary.

Joseph sipped his coffee and readied a quick appearance change. He surveyed his disguise choices. He didn't want anything outstanding—didn't think there would be any reason for them to be under surveillance. Simple dark mustache and slick down the hair more than usual. Add black-rimmed geek glasses and dark brown contacts. When he finished dressing in a pullover sweater and dark slacks, he looked like an older computer nerd. He considered omitting the mustache, then decided to leave it. It might be something someone would remember.

He slipped a black onyx ring on his right ring finger. If he couldn't be identified otherwise, this was the final item of confirmation.

A shallow box contained the brooch, so the Buyer could inspect it without displaying it for all to see. Now he checked it himself, something he hadn't taken time to do.

It was old and heavy. Crafted of gold, it was, he supposed, a replica of the sun. The center was a large round circle, a little over an inch in diameter, with six points jutting out from the center. Smooth, no other decorations, except one of the points had a notch in it. He flipped it over in his hand. It was ugly—he looked closer to see if carats were inscribed on it. He didn't see anything and wasn't about to dig out magnifiers. He turned it again and inspected the front of it. This was a brooch the jeweler was working on to switch back to what? Piece of gold that looked like the sun? Who would ever wear this? It was big and clumsy and ugly. It looked more like a decoration for a lady's jewelry box. He understood the jeweler was supposed to fix the unprofessional work previously done by another jeweler.

Joseph returned the piece to the shallow box and checked his time again. Forty-five minutes. He completed dressing, slipped his laptop and brooch into his briefcase, and headed to the tiny combo living room and kitchen. He collected a little bag of garbage.

No other tenants stirred as he dropped the trash into the local dumpster for the complex. The morning was quiet as he slid into his sedan.

The café was situated in the parking lot of the larger mall in the city. The lot looked relatively full; early morning workers stopped off for a quick coffee, and checked some stock changes, e-mails, and texts. Some customers had brought their own wireless laptops and were busy staring at screens or typing intermittently. There was the hum of idle chatter between customers.

This is good. Joseph looked typical of the clientele. He kept a wary eye on the security cameras and averted his face to keep facial recognition difficult, if not impossible. He ordered a large latte and a plain bagel with cream cheese. An unoccupied booth on the outer wall beckoned to him. He didn't know what the Buyer looked like but knew he would wear black, with a beige coat slung over his left arm.

He placed the latte and bagel on the table. The briefcase he set on the seat between himself and the wall. He took a bite of his bagel and checked the clientele again. No newcomers arrived. Joseph turned, opened his briefcase, extracted a small laptop, and placed it before him. It was smaller than he preferred, but it had quick access to his bank and would display immediately when the Buyer's money was wired into his account. Due to its small size, it was easy to transport. He powered it up, confirmed his virtual privacy network was in place and all security measures were operating. It was ready to jump at his command.

He checked his watch again. The Buyer should arrive anytime.

Joseph sipped his coffee and finished the last bite of his bagel when the Buyer appeared. Joseph rested his elbow on the table, raising his right hand to adjust his laptop, making the onyx ring clearly visible. The Buyer nodded briefly as one acquaintance to another and placed his order at the counter.

His coffee in hand, he strolled to Joseph's booth and sat opposite him. There were no other customers on either side of the men.

The Buyer was tall and fair-haired, his hairline tending toward baldness in the front. Light blue eyes were deep set in a face altogether too pale.

Joseph wondered if the Buyer had health issues. Since this was the only time he intended to see this man, he quickly dismissed any thoughts concerning his health. He'd talked to him a few times on the phone. Now that he met him, Joseph intended this to be the end of their relationship.

"Hey, man, how ya doin'?" The Buyer greeted Joseph in the manner of a congenial co-worker. Another patron would conclude it was two businessmen discussing business before they went their separate ways for the day.

"Doin' fine, buddy," Joseph answered. He didn't have a real name for the Buyer. "Did you catch the OU/OSU game over the weekend?"

"No, I didn't get in until it was all over. Heard OU won. That's good." He set his briefcase on the table and opened it so that the back was to the aisle. His laptop was situated in the middle of the case, and he pulled out a manila folder with a spreadsheet on top of it. The Buyer handed it to Joseph and said, "Here's the information you requested. Do you have what I need?"

"Right here." Joseph reached down to his briefcase on the seat beside him. He pulled out the shallow box holding the brooch and placed it inside another manila folder. He also brought out some paperwork that looked official and passed it along with the folder to the Buyer.

Joseph pretended to study the spreadsheet sent with

his folder while the Buyer opened the manila folder. Away from any prying eyes, if there were any, he scrutinized the sun brooch. His face slowly broke into a wide smile.

"Ah, yes, this is it, this is it!" The Buyer carefully inspected all the edges of the piece and extracted a small magnifying glass from his pocket. He studied all sides, back and front, of the piece. He then took a much-folded and handled piece of paper out of his pocket. It was a life-size replica of the brooch, identical in shape and size, which the man measured against the real object. He placed the paper with the sun on top of it, exact in every detail.

The Buyer put the box back together and slipped it into his coat pocket. "Well, in looking over this information you've given me, I think all is in order. Give me a few minutes to enter this into my system." He turned to his laptop and typed.

Joseph studied the paperwork he was holding again as though he wasn't quite finished with it. "This looks good, too," he said as he refreshed his screen.

The Buyer stopped typing for a moment and pulled out another file. He handed it to Joseph. "Here's another file you might want to consider, as we discussed previously." His eyes were void as he passed it to Joseph.

Joseph reached for the folder and opened it. Inside was an envelope that was to contain fifty thousand dollars cash. The arrangement was for fifty thousand cash, four hundred fifty thousand wired to his bank. Joseph discreetly scanned the café before looking inside the cash envelope. His experienced eye told him all was there.

The Buyer finished typing. "There, that's done," he

said as though he had finished a report. He looked at the fake information spreadsheet and file he handed previously to Joseph. "Do you think you want to keep that file?" he asked innocently, as though they were discussing the morning workload.

"Let me just check something," Joseph replied as he pulled up his bank records. There it was: four hundred fifty thousand new dollars in his account. This had gone smoother than he expected. It appeared the Buyer had been straight with him. "Yes, I think I will keep it." He confirmed and closed the laptop. He placed it, with the fake paperwork, in his briefcase.

Both laptops were in their briefcases, and the men finished their morning coffee. They rose to leave.

Joseph felt pretty good. *I might take a few days off. Go to the Hamptons. It's pretty this time of year. Or maybe the mountains before the snow falls.* Early retirement was still a consideration.

The Buyer stood, walked to the trash bin, and deposited his empty coffee cup. After he did so, he returned to Joseph, his face solemn. He whispered. "You no doubt heard they're looking for a person of interest in that jewelry store murder yesterday."

Joseph kept his gaze steady, freezing a poker face. This was not on the morning news he and Al had watched.

The Buyer watched Joseph for a reaction. If there was a witness, that was Joseph's problem. "Well. Have a good day, buddy. See ya later." They both knew there would be no later. That was just added for the benefit of anyone listening. He turned and walked out of the café.

Joseph suddenly had the desire to buy the morning paper. Al had read the newspaper in the apartment and

44

said there was no mention of a person of interest. Was it a Tulsa paper or a different paper? Joseph couldn't remember. He picked up his trash and briefcase and went to the front of the café where he bought a Tulsa and Oklahoma City paper. Putting both under his arm, he hurried to the car, intent on returning to his apartment to peruse them and see if he had something or someone to worry about.

Chapter Five

Emma muddled through her Friday workday without any major blunders, her stress level increasing by the hour. By the end of the day, she decided the companionship and advice of her best friends were needed. She texted Tina and Jan while on break and arranged dinner and drinks at one of their favorite haunts.

However, by the end of the night, Emma felt worse, not better. Tina had been dumped by her boyfriend of two years, and Jan was afraid she was about to lose her job. They were both absorbed in their own troubles. She found no opportunity to voice her worries.

When Saturday morning dawned, Emma woke surly and achy. Her eyes were gritty as she slowly made her way to the bathroom. Marms weaved in front of her as she stumbled along, making the trek more difficult. He insisted on walking with her, yowling the whole time. She told him to go into the kitchen and wait for her. As usual, he paid no attention.

She looked at her reflection in the mirror. Had she forgotten to take her contacts out the night before? No, they were in their case. She washed her face and eyes. *It's a new day. I should feel better.*

Marms had given up talking and was giving her the silent treatment, glaring. His tail swished in agitation.

"All right, all right." She patted her face dry and swabbed on moisturizer. She made her way to the kitchen, Marms at her heels. By the time she opened his food bag, he was circling impatiently at his dish.

Emma decided a fast-food breakfast was needed. She threw on a clean T-shirt, jeans, and flip flops, and headed down the apartment stairs to her car.

As she climbed the steps to her apartment with her order, her cell phone rang. It was her mother, probably wanting to know if she still had an upset stomach. Emma had forgotten to call her mother back yesterday. Mom had not.

Sighing, she set her food on the counter and answered the phone, hoping the call wouldn't take long.

"Hi, honey." Mom sounded serious or worried. "Are you feeling better?"

"Yeah, I'm okay." Emma began to unwrap her food in anticipation of a short conversation.

"You got something in the mail today. Are you doing all right with your bills? Are you seriously behind on anything?" Her mother had that *I want to help, but I don't want to pry* tone to her voice.

Emma was puzzled. "I'm doing okay. Why? What came in the mail?"

"Well, it's from an attorney, and I couldn't think of anything else it could be. Do you want me to open it?"

"Sure, go ahead. Tell me what it says. What attorney?"

She heard her mother slicing open the envelope. Apparently, she had an opener handy, ready to use. "It's an attorney in Grove. Johnson, Johnson, and Hale." There was silence, and Emma envisioned her mom scanning the letter.

"It's from Paul Johnson. He wants to see you in his office as soon as possible. Something about Mr.

Kerwood's will. Any of this sound familiar?"

"Uh, actually, it does." Emma pushed her sandwich aside, her appetite forgotten. "Read me the whole letter, please."

She listened while her mom read the brief letter, word for word. As she finished, her mother said, "This sounds like it may be a good thing. There's a phone number at the bottom. I'm sure they're not open today, being Saturday, but maybe you could leave a message. Say when you could be there."

"Yeah. I think I'll do that." Emma hesitated; her mind raced. "Let me come out and get that letter. I just want to see it in person. Then I'll call him."

"And will you tell me what this is all about?"

"Yeah, I'll tell you. It's pretty weird. See you in a little bit." She hung up and grabbed her purse along with her drink and sandwich. She would eat in the car. Emma was anxious to read this letter.

****

"So that's it, as best as I can figure." Emma sat at her parents' table in the breakfast nook, the attorney's letter in her hand, the remains of her drink in front of her. She told her mother about the funeral and meeting Mr. Johnson there. They both figured her presence at the funeral had something to do with the will. She had conveniently left out the part about the jewelry store robbery and murder, only starting at the part where she'd gone to the funeral.

She hoped her mom wouldn't think it was odd that she attended a funeral for a person she didn't know in the middle of a workday.

No such luck. Her mom was puzzled. "But why were *you* there? You didn't know him? And funerals take time, wouldn't you miss work? Was that okay with your boss?"

Fortunately, Emma had time to conceive a white lie to circumvent her mother's questioning. "I knew of him from the firm. I went as a representative." She nodded as she spoke, avoiding her parent's eyes. "It was recommended that I go."

Her mother wouldn't let go so easily. "Someone in the firm knew him? Why didn't they go?"

"They were in court." That was always a good excuse for an attorney to be away from the office. Being in court could take an hour or all day, depending on how things went. "I was the best person to send at the time." When her mom still looked doubtful, she said, "It was okay, Mom. Just let it go. Now I'm gonna call Mr. Johnson and leave a message that I would like to come in Monday afternoon. I'm sure Mr. James will let me leave a couple of hours early, even on short notice. I've hardly taken any time off since I started."

Emma phoned the number in the letter and began to leave her message. She was surprised when, shortly after leaving her name, a man's voice interrupted her message.

"Miss Stone? Paul Johnson. We met at the funeral." After a few words, she recognized the smooth voice.

"Oh. I really didn't expect to talk to anyone today." Emma paused. "I got your letter, and I'm a little confused."

"I'm glad you called—I'm in the office doing some catch-up work. If we could meet as soon as possible, I'll be glad to clear up any confusion. Would it be possible to meet today? I'm going to be here for a while and could be here longer if you could come to the office."

"Today?" Emma shot a questioning look at her

mother, who heard enough to know Emma was no longer leaving a message but had reached a live person. She was unashamedly eavesdropping, watching Emma, and trying her best to determine both sides of the conversation. She shrugged her shoulders as if to say, "Why not?"

"You're in Grove, right?" Emma glanced down at the letter. "I'm at least an hour, maybe two, away from your office." She wasn't sure she wanted to make that kind of drive on such short notice. She planned on a lazy afternoon.

Mr. Johnson was sympathetic. However, he pressed the issue. "This can wait until later, but I would urge you to come and visit with me as soon as possible. It will be to your advantage."

Her mom was motioning to her. "Go!" she whispered. "What else were you going to do today? It can't hurt!"

Emma sighed. Her mom's enthusiasm was contagious. "All right."

She looked at her watch. "It's noon now. I'll try to be there around two-ish." She looked down at her faded T-shirt, jeans with the hole at the knee, and flip-flops. "Guess you're pretty informal on a Saturday, aren't you? I'm not exactly dressed for an attorney's office."

He chuckled. "Yes, very informal." He gave the address that matched the letterhead, complete with directions. He asked her to call if she had any problems finding the office and said he wouldn't leave before she got there.

She hung up and looked at her mom, who waited in anticipation. "So, what's happening?"

"I don't know. But I'm off to Grove to see an

attorney."

****

Emma drove directly to the attorney's office. Built into the line of buildings and businesses along the main street, she found it easily. She parked her compact, hit the lock button on her keychain, and walked to the entrance. She ran her fingers through her hair, pulled it back behind her ears, and straightened her purse on her shoulder. As she got to the door, she tugged on her old T-shirt so that it would come down over the edge of her jeans.

Mr. Johnson's smiling face greeted her as he opened the door. "I looked out and saw you. Please come in. I'm glad you could come today." He motioned her inside, and Emma stepped into the cool lobby of his law firm. He held his hand out for a handshake, and Emma obliged.

"Well, I was curious. You said this was to my advantage, and here I am." Emma showed a hesitant smile.

"Yes. Please, sit down. Would you like coffee, soda?" He indicated a large office to the side. An old mahogany desk dominated the room, littered with legal papers. Emma followed and took a seat in an overstuffed, comfortable chair facing the desk. "No, I'm fine."

Like most attorney offices, the furnishings and decorations were expensive. Mr. Johnson's bookcase across the back wall behind his desk was full of the typical law books. Some were in disarray, as though they had been in recent use and hadn't been put back in their correct place. Others looked as though they were essential but had not been touched in a long time. Somehow, Emma didn't think this was a firm that specialized in divorce cases. However, Grove was a small town. She didn't know what law they practiced here.

Mr. Johnson spoke, and Emma redirected her wandering mind.

"…so glad you could make it today. There are some things we cannot accomplish today, but we can get a good start, and you can start making plans for yourself." Mr. Johnson shuffled and rearranged things on his desk. Emma assumed to make room for paperwork as to her reason for being there.

"Excuse me? Making plans? Can we back up a bit, as I don't really know *why* I'm here." Emma slipped her purse off her shoulder and leaned forward.

"Of course, of course! I apologize. I know why you're here and forgot that you did not. I'm not usually so disorganized." He piled the paperwork neatly at the side. He pulled out another file from a drawer at the side bottom of his desk. It was bulky, but neat, little colored tabs sticking out of the side, attached to their own respective papers.

Mr. Johnson sat the file in front of him, crossed his hands over it, and leaned forward, his full attention devoted to Emma. "You are here because of the last will and testament of Jonathan Louis Kerwood. You are named as a beneficiary in his will."

"Excuse me?" Confused, Emma said, "I'm sure you have figured out by now that I was not, uh…" *Don't mess up what could be a good thing here, Emma.* "I was not very close to Mr. Kerwood."

"I have figured that out." Mr. Johnson, with a slight smile on his face, nodded. "But that, however, is beside the point. Let me read you his will, and we'll discuss it."

His voice began to intone the usual beginnings of a will, and Emma listened, her curiosity piqued. It appeared Mr. Kerwood was quite a wealthy man, had no known relatives and no friends he felt generous toward. There were three other people mentioned in the will, but they had been provided for elsewhere, so they were not necessary to be present when the will was being read. Only Emma was there, and apparently, her part came in where the will read "the remainder and entirety of my estate shall be distributed amongst those who attend my funeral. I depend on the honesty and integrity of the law firm of Johnson, Johnson, and Hale to keep this condition of my will strictly private. Any acquaintances, employees, friends, and relatives associated with anyone in that law firm or the funeral home is barred from receipt of any portion of my estate. The law firm of Johnson, Johnson, and Hale and the funeral home have been compensated for their part in this last will and testament."

There were following parts in the will, but they did not concern any other inheritance or parties involved, and Emma spaced it out. When Mr. Johnson finally finished reading, he looked up to see Emma, a glazed look on her face. He smiled and said, "So, Miss Stone, simply put, you have inherited a fortune."

****

Emma accepted the cold can of cola Mr. Johnson handed her. He explained they didn't normally keep her preferred brand, so he was unable to provide her with that. His short walk to get the cola had been enough time for Emma's mind to spring up with questions.

She took a sip, set it down, then verbally spewed, using her hands and shaking her head at the same time.

"I don't get it; these things just don't happen. I mean, how can I be the only one who inherits all this man's wealth? I didn't even know him."

"You were the only one that came to his funeral. It's that simple."

"Okay, okay. But he was a rich man. This is a small town. When people knew he died, wouldn't some come for the, you know...morbid curiosity?"

"Mr. Kerwood specified prior to his death, when he died, he did not want a notice in the paper until *after* the funeral. Since the funeral was held within two days after his death, there was no problem keeping it out of the newspaper. He was very much what you would call a recluse."

"So, how can you be a recluse and be this rich?" This seemed beyond Emma's comprehension. "Wouldn't people always be trying to get money from you for charities or something?"

"Mr. Kerwood handled all matters of charities through us. He only saw his nurse, his housekeeper, and the gardener on a regular basis, all of whom he employed full time and are the others mentioned in his will that he provided for otherwise."

"Just how rich was he? What exactly have I inherited?"

Mr. Johnson had a slight *you're gonna like this* smile on his face. He shuffled papers as he picked one to read to her. "This is rather a rough estimate as we are still compiling figures, but there is a portfolio of two point six million in stocks and bonds, one hundred thousand cash in a bank in Tulsa, two savings accounts over a hundred grand each, fifty-five thousand in a local bank, and the estate of one hundred acres with a rather large home on one of the higher points overlooking Grand Lake, in Grove." He watched Emma's face as she tried to absorb the information. She was turning white, and he hoped she wasn't going to faint.

"We can see the property today if you would like." He interjected, hoping to keep her thoughts with him. Perhaps it was a bit much for her to absorb all at once. "As to money in the bank, I will need to take you to the bank personally, draw up a signature card for the accounts, and attend to paperwork."

Emma seldom had more than a ten-dollar bill in her pocket and lived paycheck to paycheck most of her young, independent life. She had borrowed money from her mom to buy gas to drive to Grove for this meeting. The thought she inherited that sum of money and property was unreal. She remembered the old adage, 'If it's too good to be true, it probably is,' and looked at the attorney.

"Are you *sure* about this? This isn't a cruel joke? There's some hidden cousin or someone going to bust out of a closet?" Emma's face had gone from white to a growing pink at the mere thought.

"I assure you, Miss Stone, this is no joke." His face solemn as he shook his head. He stood up behind his desk. "Now. Would you like to see your property?"

Chapter Six

Officers on street patrol canvassed the businesses. They did not locate their elusive witness. Starting Thursday afternoon, as soon as photos were printed, and Friday, with no leads. There were a couple of attorney offices they missed because they stopped at lunchtime, and they were closed. Other businesses they tried didn't recognize the girl.

Mike returned to the office to check if anything new came from forensics to help identify the killer, with or without a witness. The victim had been shot (which they knew) by a nine-millimeter (which they figured), but there was nothing additional.

Mrs. Sun and the daughter who helped run the jewelry store checked the inventory, and nothing for sale was missing. As for any pieces that were to be repaired, they weren't sure. Mrs. Sun explained her husband sometimes took in special pieces and kept information to himself. Perhaps he had something to work on, and it was specified that no one else should touch it.

His phone rang, and it was his excitable partner. "Mike! I'm bringing in a guy that runs a funeral home. He might know our witness."

A funeral home? He'd take anything at this point. "Great. I'll be here when you get here."

"On our way. Just a few minutes, and we'll be there."

****

Brad Thomas walked into the police station ahead of Jim Jeffries. Jim practically bounced in his excitement. Mike frowned at him, and he managed to curb his enthusiasm. "Mr. Thomas, this is my partner, Mike Wells."

"Please, have a seat." It was quiet in the detective division, and there were few other officers in the large sprawling room. Jim hitched his leg up and propped his hip against Mike's desk, earning another sour look from Mike. Jim looked eagerly at Thomas and ignored his partner.

A picture of Emma was put forward. "Mr. Thomas, we appreciate you coming in. Can you tell us anything about this young woman?"

Brad Thomas glanced at the picture and looked uncomfortable. "She seemed like a very nice young lady—I really hope she's not in trouble." He paused as if to consider what he was about to say. "And maybe, after all, I should refer you to the attorney who will represent her. He may not want me to give her information."

"Mr. Thomas. The young woman is not here, and neither is her attorney. I don't see an attorney for you, and you aren't being charged with anything. We just want information." He looked Thomas in the eye, his impatience showing. "We know her as Emma. Do you know her full name?"

"Her name is Emma Stone."

"Do you know her address?"

"It's back at the office. I remember she gave an address in Broken Arrow."

"She doesn't work for you?" This had been Mike's assumption.

"No. She attended a funeral." At Mike's questioning expression, he continued. "A funeral for Jonathan Louis Kerwood last Thursday afternoon."

Bingo! "When did she arrive at the funeral home?"

"The funeral was at two, and she arrived just before."

"Was she alone? Did she seem upset, distraught?"

Thomas looked thoughtful. "She was alone. She seemed a little flustered, but people show a lot of different emotions at funerals. Nothing really weird." He shrugged.

"Let's get her address so we can reach her." He pushed the desk phone toward Thomas, an invitation to call his office and get Emma's address. When he did so, Mike thanked him and asked an officer to give him a ride back to the funeral home.

Mike waved the address at Jim. "Let's make a little trip to Broken Arrow."

****

Detective Mike Wells and his partner Jim Jeffries stood outside the door of the sprawling ranch home, identified as the home of Emma Stone. They rang the doorbell and waited.

The door was opened by a middle-aged woman wiping her hands on a dishtowel. She hesitated but smiled. "Can I help you?"

"Ma'am, I'm Detective Mike Wells of the Tulsa police, and this is my partner, Jim Jeffries. Is Emma Stone here? We'd like to speak with her."

"Umm," was all Emma's mother managed to say.

Her husband walked up behind her. "What's going on?" He had just come home and hadn't learned of Emma's visit earlier or what she had told her mother.

"Come in, officers. I'm Kay Stone, Emma's mother. This is my husband, Jack." She waved for them to come in. "Emma's not here right now, and I'm not sure when she'll return or when we'll hear from her. What's going on? Is she in trouble?"

"We can't really comment at this time, ma'am, but we need to speak with her." As the worried look on the woman's face did not go away, Mike continued. "Actually, we think she may have witnessed a crime, and what information she can give us could be crucial to our investigation."

"Oh, my. When was this?" Her mother was having one of those feelings of intuition mothers are famous for, and she didn't like it.

Since no answers had been forthcoming, her husband was still mystified. "What's this about? Kay?"

She didn't answer but continued to observe the detective, who had identified himself as Mike Wells. He hadn't answered her. "When was this crime?"

"Early Thursday afternoon."

"Would someone please tell me what's going on? Is Emma mixed up in something?" asked Mr. Stone.

Kay turned to her husband. "I think this may have something to do with why Emma went to Grove today."

"Grove?" Her husband was still confused. "Oklahoma?"

"Yes, honey, Grove, Oklahoma."

"Why Grove? We don't know anyone there." He looked at the officers as though they could explain it. They returned blank stares.

"I don't know. But she got a letter from an attorney, and she went to Grove to meet him at his office."

"Let's back up a bit." They'd wandered into the

living room, and Detective Wells was trying to get the pieces together. No one seemed to know what they were talking about, but he determined Kay Stone understood the most. "Emma got a letter. From an attorney. In Grove."

"Yes." Kay turned an open face to the detective. "He wanted her to meet him today if possible, so she went there earlier. I haven't heard back from her."

"Is he representing her? This attorney?"

"I don't know. Does he need to?" Again, the concerned, worried look on Kay's face.

"Okay. Back up again." Mike decided to start over. "Did she contact this attorney?"

"After he sent the letter to her, yes." Kay frowned.

"So, he contacted her first?" At Kay's nod, he continued. "Do you know *why* he sent the letter to her?"

"Oh. It had something to do with a funeral she attended and a will."

"Funeral?" Jack's mind had wandered, but "funeral" caught his attention. "Somebody she knew died?" His brow furrowed. "Someone we knew?"

"No, dear, nobody we knew, and I don't think she knew him either." The three men stared at her, waiting for an explanation. She motioned them toward the couch and chairs. "This is a little confusing, but let me tell you what she said." She revealed the story Emma told her of going to Mr. Kerwood's funeral as a representative of the firm.

"I'm beginning to doubt if that's the real reason she went to that funeral; however, I cannot for the life of me see how going to a funeral is tied in with a crime she may have witnessed." Kay finished with this explanation, looking at the detectives as though they should be able to explain it.

Detective Wells spoke. "We don't know either, Mrs. Stone, but we would really like to talk to Emma."

"Well, she took the letter with her. But the attorney was a Mr. Johnson, with Johnson, Johnson, and Hale in Grove. I'll give you Emma's cell number."

Detective Wells stated they would like that, and Jim pulled out a notepad and scribbled it down.

The phone rang, and Mrs. Stone reached for it. "That's Emma now."

Emma was excitedly babbling.

"Wait, wait, wait, honey, slow down!" Kay tried to get Emma to stop so she could get a word in and tell her she was urgently being sought by the police. Both detectives had followed her to the phone, and Mike indicated for her to hand it to him.

Emma paused for breath when her mom's voice broke through her excitement. "Honey, stop a minute. There are a couple of men here who really need to speak to you, really bad. It's important. Understand?"

Emma listened and immediately reached the worst conclusion: the killer had tracked her down and was holding her parents hostage. "Oh no. Mom, are you okay? Have they hurt you? What do they want?"

Kay held the phone out from her ear and looked at it, puzzled. Had she heard her daughter correctly? Why would the police hurt them? "We're fine, sweetie. But there are police detectives here who want to talk to you. Can you talk to them now?"

At Detective Wells' impatient look, Kay figured her daughter better talk regardless. "Actually, honey, I'm going to put Detective Wells on the phone. Here he is." She handed the phone to him.

"Emma Stone? This is Detective Mike Wells with the Tulsa police department. I talked briefly with you on Thursday afternoon. My partner and I would really like to speak with you about…" He glanced over; Emma's parents were hanging on his every word.

"…the robbery and murder you witnessed this week."

He waited for her reply and received a meek "Okay."

"This is important. What you tell us may help us catch the perpetrator of this horrible crime." When no further comment came from Emma, he continued, "When are you coming back? We would like to meet with you in person as soon as possible."

"I was thinking of spending the night in Grove, but I can come back any time. Could you wait until morning?"

"We'd prefer not to. We'd rather talk to you when your memory is fresh and a couple of days have passed already."

"All right. Let me finish up a few things with the attorney, and I'll be there. I'll call you when I'm back, and you can direct me where to meet. Do I have to come to the police station?"

"It would be preferable. It shouldn't take long. We just want to go over what you saw." He gave her his cell phone number. "Call me when you're almost here."

He disconnected and turned to his partner. "It'll be a couple of hours before she's here. We might as well get some early dinner." He looked at Kay and Jack, who stood, as outsiders wanting to come in. "And we can let these fine people get back to their lives." Mike apologized for taking up their time as he and Jim turned to leave.

"Whoa, whoa, just a minute." Kay stepped in front of both detectives. Her husband stood behind them, eyes wide, motioning her to leave them alone. She couldn't. Not yet. "What has Emma witnessed? You think she saw someone *kill someone*?" She shook her head, "I don't believe it. She didn't say a word about it. She would have told me."

Detective Wells gently nudged her to the side as he pushed the door open. "It may be more complicated than you think, Mrs. Stone. Emma may have several reasons for not telling you, and we don't know how much she saw. Once we know what she *did* see, we may request she not tell anyone, including *you*." He inclined his head toward her. "Have a nice evening, folks." He continued toward their unmarked car.

Jim had managed to ease past Mrs. Stone and opened his door. "What do you think?" he asked as Mike slid behind the wheel.

"I think she'll talk to us tonight, now that we've found her." He started the car. "I fully expect a phone call in about two hours."

"So why didn't she call earlier?"

"Scared. There's a killer out there, and she knows it. But since we've resumed contact with her, she knows we can find her. I doubt she'll try to slip away again. How does Mexican sound?"

Chapter Seven

Emma hung up her cell phone and sighed. *Darn!* They were in Mr. Johnson's plush sedan, as he drove her to the house she had "inherited." That word still seemed alien to her; she should inherit something as grand as he had described. The police had found her and were pushing her to talk to them. For all her worry and indecision, she was a little relieved. She had to go to the police; they knew where to find her.

Mr. Johnson was aware something was going on that his client didn't like, but he asked no questions. He drove down the highway, headed out of town. He figured Ms. Stone would tell him in her own time. Which was immediately.

"I need to get back to Tulsa right away." She heaved a heavy sigh of frustration. "We'll have to tour the house another time."

"Well, you can see it from the outside, and if you want to return early next week, we can wrap up a few more details. I'll take you to the bank and the house, and introduce you to the caretaker and housekeeper, in case you'd like to keep them as employees. That sort of thing." He continued in the same direction, with no indication of turning around. "We're almost there. You can get an idea of the place."

Surely, the detectives can wait another few minutes or hour, depending on what needs to be done back at Mr.

Johnson's office. He hasn't indicated there's much, but he seems anxious to have me see the house.

"Did Mr. Kerwood live in the house with just the housekeeper and caretaker?"

"Yes, and the nurse he employed full time. He passed away in the house, absolutely hated hospitals. Otherwise, he lived by himself. Mrs. O'Malley has been his housekeeper and cook for around fifteen years, and Mr. O'Malley has been his caretaker and gardener for even longer. There are three small cottages on the property, and they live in one of them. The nurse, Nancy Karroll, lives in another of the cottages. The third is vacant, and Ms. Karroll is planning on moving soon. Mr. Kerwood provided them the cottages free of charge. He wanted to keep his help close by, especially in his later years." As an afterthought, he added, "Mr. Kerwood was generous with the grocery bill, so they also had plenty of free food, provided Mrs. O'Malley was willing to cook it."

"That sounds like a pretty good deal—free food, free rent. Were they, like, required to be at his beck and call? Like, all the time?" Emma was thinking back to the days of servants, cooks, and butlers; hadn't she read that a day off was a luxury?

"Oh, no. They worked a regular workweek. Mr. Kerwood usually made his own way on weekends, as I understand it. He did occasionally call the nurse in on weekends, but not often."

"What will they do now? Are they looking for work?"

"Mr. Kerwood left them a hefty savings account. He also had property near the other side of town, which he already deeded to them. Should they wish, they have enough to build a comfortable home there." With a sideways glance, he added, "But I think the O'Malleys were hoping to continue on at the estate for a while longer." He glanced over at her. "That is up to you."

She stared out the car window, watching the slightly rolling green hills slide by. They had crossed over the lake, viewing some of the prettiest scenery in the area, with the lake and hills serene under the blue Oklahoma sky. She wondered if this decision would be handled for her as easily as the last difficult one had been. And darn! If that thought didn't bring back other horrible memories of the day she walked into that jewelry store. For a while today, she'd had pleasant, exciting thoughts.

Emma moved on her seat cushion and readjusted her position as she reviewed her thoughts. *Right now, I cannot do anything about what will happen later today. Right now, I will go look at my property and shall go from there. Period.* She dismissed her worries for later and plastered a contented look on her face.

Turning to Mr. Johnson, she said, "So the property is one hundred acres, on a hill, and it has three houses on it?"

"Four, actually. The main house and three cottages. The cottages are for the caretakers or guests. They each sit on a small lot and have two bedrooms and a bath. They are situated in the rear of the property so there's privacy for all parties."

"O-kay…" Emma drew out the *kay* as her mind raced. "Just how big is the main house?" she asked Mr. Johnson.

"You should be able to see it in just a couple of minutes." He flipped on the signal to make a left off the highway onto a narrow paved roadway. A wrought iron fence surrounded it, and a sign hung on the fence by the entrance, clearly stating it was *Private Property*. A well-cared-for landscape appeared, and a narrow road wound up the side of the hill.

"If you know what to look for, you can see it from the highway." He executed a rather tight little curve. "The house itself is three stories, although the third story has been closed off for years, and Mr. Kerwood would have closed off the second story, but the way the house is constructed would have been difficult. He made the den on the first floor into his bedroom, so the main floor has been his living quarters for the last several years. Now, we'll see your property after we go around this next curve."

They rounded the curve, and there was her new home. Emma leaned forward in her seat, unaware that her mouth hung open. The sight was more than her eyes could take in at once.

It was truly one of the most beautiful homes and settings she had ever seen. It rivaled movies and documentaries of places where the truly rich or famous lived, but nothing she had ever hoped to own. For the moment, she didn't even consider that this was hers. She sat and let the fabulous sight soak in.

It was a beautiful three-story mansion, primarily of light-colored stone blocks, a solid rectangular design. A central entrance stood out from the front of the home, rising all three stories, giving the slight appearance of a castle. Large windows (she liked that) were arranged symmetrically, giving an even, pleasant appearance. She could only assume that the rooms inside were also evenly aligned. The overall appearance of the home was comforting and whispered, "Welcome." Clean lines, strong façade. It was breathtaking to her. The narrow road drove directly up to the house, circling around in the front. Three large circular steps led up to the main portico. An iron bench, complete with cushions, provided an additional sense of welcome.

There were trees along the drive, but not in the front of the house, as though the house wanted to claim all the attention and not share in the glory with mere trees. Neatly clipped shrubs in the front and along the sides, encompassed the building. The steps rose to the seven-foot double doors in the central entrance.

Emma didn't realize she had been holding her breath. "Ohmigosh," she whispered. "This is so beautiful." She let out a long breath. She looked over at Mr. Johnson, who was admiring the house also. "Am I dreaming? Is this for real?"

He chuckled. "I assure you, Miss Stone, this is for real. You are a very lucky young lady." He held up a key ring with several keys dangling from it. "Do you want to take time for a quick tour? Or do you need to get back to Tulsa?"

What she wanted to do was snatch those keys from him, make a dash for the front door, and hide from the realities she had to face later. She shook her head. "No. If this is real, it's not going anywhere. Right?" She shot a look across at him, and he shook his head.

"No, it will be right here. It was built in forty-five and hasn't moved since."

"Chance it might burn down?"

"Not likely."

"Tornado come through and rip it up?"

"None predicted."

"Offbeat cousins show up out of the blue and usurp

me?"

He looked at her in surprise. "We already discussed cousins in closets. No usurping likely."

She smiled. "You might be surprised. Sure no usurpers?"

"No usurpers. The will is clear."

She looked again at the mansion. She wanted to go inside so bad.

Her mother's voice echoed in her head. *Don't let something that you have to do hang over your head. Get it done. Then you can play.* She had delayed her talk with the police long enough. It would not do to antagonize the detective by further delays. She knew this was the best course of action, so she gritted her teeth and made up her mind.

"Take me back to the office, please, and I'll head to Tulsa and do what needs to be done."

As he pulled the car around the front of the house to follow the circle drive and leave, she asked, "When can I come back?"

"I would recommend Monday. That way, we can also take care of the bank business since it will be a business day."

"Fine. I'll be back Monday afternoon. I do still have a job, and I would like to talk to my boss before I take off."

"You realize the income from the estate makes it unnecessary that you have work."

"I kind of figured." She paused for a moment. "But my folks drilled it into me that I should never suddenly leave a job. I did when I was a teenager. I've not had this position very long, and I like it. The people are nice, and I don't want to leave them in a bind."

"That's very mature of you." They drove on in silence. He concentrated on the narrow roadway while Emma's mind filled with thoughts of what she would tell the police. Before she knew it, they had arrived at the attorney's office.

"So I will plan on seeing you Monday afternoon, Miss Emma Stone." He smiled as they shook hands in parting. "I have no afternoon appointments and nothing in court that day."

"Good. If I have anything come up, I'll call you. In fact, I may call just to make sure this is all real. Would you mind?" Emma was thinking she might still need to do a reality check before she made any decisions about her present job.

"Not in the least. Call anytime you like." He fished out a business card from his wallet and wrote his cell number on the back. "Just in case you can't reach me at the office," he said.

Emma took the card, and they said goodbyes again. He went inside to finish the paperwork. Emma started her car to return to the city, the police, and their questions.

As she drove west, she recalled her brief conversation with the detective. To her surprise, he had not sounded mad. He had to know she had delayed going to the police on purpose, and she expected at the very least a short chastising. But maybe that was still to come. She couldn't blame him if he did chew her out. *Maybe, when I explain, he'll understand.*

Chapter Eight

Emma dialed Detective Wells's cell phone. She was nervous about talking to the detective. *But I didn't do anything wrong, except avoid calling him.* She had only done that because she was scared about the killer finding her.

"So, I'm just going to tell him the truth." Emma spoke out loud as she nodded her head and waited for Detective Wells to answer. When he did, she told him who she was and asked for directions to the station.

"Where are you?" Mike asked before giving her detailed instructions. He said he would meet her on the ground floor of the police station.

Mike hung up and noted the time. He busied himself with cleaning dirty coffee cups and some leftover napkins from breakfast and straightened his paperwork. At least part of his desktop was visible.

His file on the jewelry store robbery and murder was in his side drawer, so he pulled it out and looked over the information. The video was in the file, and he thought about showing it to Stone, if she tried to pull any lies on him. He figured he would play that by ear. He looked over what forensics sent. The bullet was from a nine-millimeter handgun retrieved and tagged as evidence. The gun was still missing. Jewelry under repair had been strewn about, and Mrs. Sun and her daughter had verified it was all there. There was a questionable piece Mr. Sun had written a ticket for, but the description was not filled in, and the only name on the ticket was *Omal*. There was also no indication of the status of the piece or payment. Mrs. Sun said her husband was not the best at keeping written records, especially on repairs. If he were doing the work and knew what was being done, he would deliver it to the owner. He didn't give information to anyone else. No one else need be involved. That was his philosophy.

Mike set the file aside and outlined the information he hoped to get from Ms. Stone. He hoped she could fill in what, when, and where. He had a few minutes and picked up the VCR tape, and ran it one more time.

She fit the description of pretty. Tall and slender, she smiled readily at Mr. Sun in the video and followed him around the display cases as he tried to sell her something.

Mike instinctively knew Emma Stone was not the killer. She was a witness and witness only. Admittedly, he was young and gaining experience, but he had seen some of the brutality men had done to their fellow man. He didn't believe Stone would shoot the old man and then steal from him. Plus, the video went off while she was in the store in full view of the cameras. No, she was just a witness, but he suspected she knew more than she realized.

Checking his watch, Mike realized Emma would pull into the parking lot momentarily. He rolled down his sleeves and shrugged into his sports coat, checking his appearance in the mirror over the water cooler. His short dark hair was sticking out at odds, but he shoved his fingers through it, then rinsed his hands in the little sink by the coffee machine. He headed to the elevator to meet his witness.

Emma approached the building as Mike reached the ground floor. He came out of the elevator and turned toward the entrance when she reached for the door. He hurried forward and pushed it open to allow her to enter.

"It's locked on weekends," he said as she edged past him.

Seeing no one else in the short hallway, she turned back to him. He checked the door to make sure it latched behind her.

Emma was about to say the polite, "Good to see you again," but it really wasn't. Instead, she stood silent. When he turned to her, she said, "Hello again," for lack of any other clever greeting.

"And hello again to you, Ms. Stone. You are not an easy person to find." He indicated the elevator. "If you would come with me, please."

About to apologize for staying under the radar, Emma hesitated, then decided silence might be her friend. So, with a tight smile, she followed the detective.

He pushed the button for the third floor. Emma held her purse at her side, simply looking at the wall as they ascended.

He's younger than I remember. Physically fit and tall, he didn't appear much older than her. Their first meeting had been warmer at the crime scene. She realized she was the reason for his chill, if indeed there was one. If she'd only tried to reach him earlier, he wouldn't need to chase her down. She glanced at him as they passed the second floor. *He does have nice eyes.*

Mike gave her a quick smile. "I bet you've had a busy couple of days. It takes effort to avoid the police." He studied her as she ignored him.

Emma looked away as she squirmed under his gaze.

"Yes," she whispered. Clearing her throat, she murmured, "It wasn't intentional. Things happened."

He shot her a quizzical glance. The elevator stopped at the third floor, and they stepped out. Detective Wells led the way to his desk in a back corner. He asked Emma if she would like soda, water, or coffee, which she declined.

She sat straight in the chair in front of his desk and looked around the large room and his paper-covered desk.

"Detective," she said as he discarded his sport coat to drape on the chair back. "I'd really like to get this over and done. I want to apologize for leaving the scene earlier and then avoiding you. Things got a little scary, and I was trying to avoid being the center of attention. I'll tell you whatever you want to know, that I can. I didn't know Mr. Sun and had never seen him before. That day, when he was shot and killed, was, well, like nothing I have ever experienced in my life. I prefer not to even think about it." Her eyes were welling with tears as she spoke.

"Then the sooner we get on with it, the sooner we're finished." The friendliness seemed to be tempered, and his demeanor serious. "I'm going to turn on the recorder." She nodded to indicate that was fine.

He turned on the machine and focused on Emma. They went through the formalities, her name, and identification.

"Okay." He leaned back in his chair, his gaze steady. Emma still sat straight and unwavering. He got the impression there was steel in her backbone.

"Let me make sure you understand. You're not under arrest. You're merely here for questioning. You are on the video of the store just before the shooting. Then the tape went dead. As we see it currently, you are a witness, and you're not under suspicion."

Emma sat straighter, her eyes wide and alert. "The video went dead? Oh my gosh, that's why he didn't seem bothered by the camera."

"You saw him then?"

"Oh yes, I got a good look at him. He looked up in the mirror at the corner of the store. I saw his face before he put his sunglasses on." She let out a long, anxious breath. She looked at Mike, her eyes angry slits and her mouth tight. "He seemed so calm after shooting that poor man. I hope you catch him."

"All right." Mike picked up a pen and his notebook. "Let's start at the beginning. Why did you go to that store on that day?"

After Emma outlined her story of the shooting, Mike asked a few more questions.

"So, you dropped your cell phone and stooped to get it when the killer came into the store?"

"Yes, and by his tone of voice at Mr. Sun, I figured I better stay down and out of sight." Embarrassed, she added, "I felt like such a coward, but I didn't know what to do."

"Don't feel bad. It saved your life, and there was nothing you could do." He looked at his notes. "So the next thing that happened, he forced the jeweler to the back room?"

"Yes. I think he was looking for something in particular. He was yelling at Mr. Sun, and I could only understand bits and pieces. I heard the word *sun*, but I thought it was Mr. Sun's name, so I don't know. But he got it because I heard him say, 'This is it!' and then there was more shuffling around or fighting, or falling, I don't know, then the shot." She was becoming more emotional as she recalled the events leading to Mr. Sun's death. Mike stepped to a co-worker's desk, returned with a handful of tissues and offered them to Emma.

"Thank you." She sorted one out and used it to wipe her wet cheeks and then daintily blew her nose while the detective waited.

"How long was it before he left?"

"Not very long—but time seemed to stand still for a while. It seemed like it happened so fast, and yet…not." She looked at him, eyes brimmed with tears. In her mind, she had moved to the next moment when she saw Mr. Sun's lifeless body.

"And you saw him leave?" He stared at her intently, willing her to sniffle up and concentrate on the man she had seen enter the shop and leave.

"Yes. I waited, I didn't move, and he came back to the front, didn't seem to be in any hurry. Before he got to the door, he stopped and put his sunglasses back on." She bit her bottom lip as a thought came to her. "I think he was waiting for someone to show up because he hesitated, then hurried out. I saw a dark car. I think it stopped, maybe giving him time to get in."

"Did you see enough of the car to identify it?"

She shook her head. "No. The store display was in the way. I only saw the nose of the car, and then it sped up." Rubbing her nose with the tissue, she added, "It was a dark four-door sedan. Older model, I think. There was a dent in the door."

"Do you think you could describe the man to an artist? We have someone who's good at computer sketching. And we have some photos you could look through."

"Sure. I've always been pretty good at faces."

Mike hoped she was stating fact. A good description of the killer would be invaluable. "After he left, what happened?"

Emma described going to the back room where the lifeless Mr. Sun lay sprawled on the floor. She sobbed but held together well. After seeing Mr. Sun and deciding he was dead, she called 911. Tears now streamed down her face.

"I had never seen a dead body before. He'd just been talking to me, and he was so nice, trying to be helpful, and this horrible man came in and yelled at him, maybe beat on him, I don't know, and then shot him." Her voice had become louder with every sentence, her eyes imploring him to understand.

"Okay, okay. You're doing really well. Very helpful." Mike leaned forward, his voice steady. He looked across his desk at her as she stifled her sobs. She was even pretty with her face all red and blotchy with tears. He mentally shook his head, clearing his thoughts. He'd like to comfort her. Instead, he rose and went to his co-worker's desk for more tissues. This time, he returned with the whole box and pushed it toward her.

She grabbed the tissues desperately, snatching a couple right away. He heard her blow her nose not so delicately as he went around the desk to finish the questioning.

A little hiccupping sound slipped out. Her shoulders shook as she tried to quiet her sobs. She looked up at him, her eyes red and swollen. "And then, I had these thoughts that you, the police, might think I killed him."

Another little sniffle and another tissue wiped her

nose. "I watch CSI, other crime shows. The person who finds the body is sometimes the first suspect."

"*Sometimes* being the keyword there." He tilted his head as he looked at her. "What would have been your motive?"

"I don't know. Robbery? He *did* take something."

"But you don't know what."

"No. I think he had it in his pocket when he left. He didn't have anything in his hands except his sunglasses."

"What about his gun? Did you see it?"

"No, but he made a—movement?—like he had put something in a shoulder holster under his left arm."

"So then what?"

"I checked on Mr. Sun. I panicked. I called 911. The rest, you know, I waited for the police to show up. You asked me a few questions, and then I left to go back to work and tell them I would be gone the rest of the afternoon."

Emma paused in her recital to remember what happened next. "Then it got kind of scary. As I went down the sidewalk, cars were going past me. It's all one way there, you know? This one car was going slow and then pulled over to park on the far side of the street. Something about it caught my eye, especially when he parked, but no one got out. By that time, I was up almost even, and I saw him. It was him, the killer!" Her breath caught as she remembered.

"I turned around and went down the first street I could and ducked beside a building. When I looked out, I saw him running toward the street where I had just come from. I ran into the first business I came to, so when I saw Thomas's Funeral Home, I went in there." This time, when she looked at him, it was with a mixture of sadness, embarrassment, and forgive-me-ness. "They were having a funeral. No one else was there, so I sat back in the family box. Hiding."

"He didn't come into the funeral home?"

"No. I didn't see him again."

After he took her statement, Mike asked Emma if she could come back in Monday morning and give a description to the artist.

"I may be able to do one better. Does she keep any art supplies here?"

"Sure." Mike stood. "Are you saying you could draw him yourself?" Mike looked at her, doubtful.

"Yes." Emma nodded in confidence. "I've always drawn family and other portraits. Not good enough to make a living at it, so I work for an attorney." She followed Mike from his office to a desk in a far corner. Off to the side was a sketch pad and a couple of charcoal pencils. He waved his hand toward the drawing materials.

"Help yourself. Marcy does a lot of her sketches on the computer, but sometimes she resorts to the old-fashioned method of drawing what people tell her."

Emma sat down in Marcy's chair and picked up the pad and pencil.

"I'll leave you alone for a few minutes so you can think and draw. Would you like that soda now?"

Emma nodded as she focused on what she needed to put on paper. "Do you have cola?"

"I believe so. Be right back." He turned and walked away to get drinks.

Emma turned her attention fully to the blank sheet in front of her. It had been a while since she had done this. It was a talent she was blessed with, and most of her family had at least one portrait or charcoal drawing on their walls. She wished she had kept her head about her and made her own drawing of the killer.

She started with the shape of the face, angular, beginning to turn a little fleshy with age. He was around middle age, in good shape, and tall with broad shoulders. She hadn't been close enough to see his eye color but remembered they were deep-set, dark. Straight dark brows, arrogant nose. Wide, generous mouth. Straight dark hair draped a little over the collar. She sketched, and his face took form on paper. *He could almost be handsome if he weren't a cold-blooded killer.*

She gave a little shiver. A coldness seeped off this man, making Emma thankful she had eluded him.

Mike returned in time to see her shudder. "Here's your drink. What's wrong?"

She looked up at his handsome face. Those blue eyes stared at her with concern. "Nothing. Just scary thoughts." She pushed the pad across to him. "I can do better if you want a more detailed sketch, but that's him." She took the soda and popped the tab as he picked up the pad. Taking a long sip, Emma closed her eyes. She didn't realize how good it would taste.

"This is incredible." Mike studied the drawing he held in his hands. "He…looks familiar." He looked at her. "You heard him speak, right? Did he have an accent?"

"I didn't notice. I might have been too scared, and he was yelling at Mr. Sun, not just talking."

Mike set the drawing down and hurried to the captain's office. He reappeared, an open book in his hands.

"Look at this—does he look like your man?" He

jabbed at a grainy picture of a dark-haired man entering a building, a scowl on the man's face.

Emma studied the picture. "Yes, that's him. Who is he?"

Mike sat back against the desk, studying first the picture and then the drawing. "He is Joseph Malone, on the top twenty of the FBI's most wanted lists. He's not dangerous, like a terrorist, and this may be the first murder he is suspected of committing. He's primarily a jewel thief. Very good, and high dollar." Mike looked at her. "He's careful not to be seen and has never been caught."

"He steals expensive jewelry?" Emma was thinking of one of her favorite old movies. The male lead from the sixties was a suave, romantic character, even though he was a criminal. This guy had the looks to go with the part. She remembered Mr. Sun. The difference was this man was a killer.

"Yes. Extremely expensive jewelry, difficult to steal. Sometimes rare pieces of art. The challenge seems to intrigue him. We believe he hires out to steal for collectors." He waved the sketch pad in the air in front of her. "This is not what he normally does. Just stealing some piece from a little jewelry store *and* killing someone in the process, not his style."

Emma finished her soda and tossed it in Marcy's trash can. "Maybe he's thinking of retirement, and this was an easy job for him."

"You may have a point." As she walked toward Mike's desk, he asked her what plans she had for the next week. "Just in case we need to call you."

"Oh my gosh, I didn't tell you! The most amazing thing!" Emma reached out and grabbed his forearm. He turned in alarm. "No, no, it's not bad, just exciting! And since it really didn't have anything to do with this, I forgot about it, except how could I really? But it happened *after* the murder…" Realizing she was babbling, she drew in a deep breath and started all over again.

"I went into the funeral home to get away from, what's his name? Joseph Malone? I sat in the family box for Mr. Kerwood's funeral. Then, I went to the graveside services. I didn't want to go back where Malone could see me. So I was gone for a few hours. Well, it turned out that I inherited his fortune. I have this big house and a lot of money from Mr. Kerwood."

Mike stared at her, his mind trying to wrap around what she garbled out to him. "This happened after the murder?"

"Yes! If I hadn't been trying to get away from Malone, I wouldn't have run into the funeral home and attended Mr. Kerwood's service. I don't know who would have gotten his money, but not me."

"You mean because you went to his funeral, you are his heir?"

Emma nodded excitedly, beaming. "It was in his will. Whoever attended his funeral inherited his fortune. I happened to be the only one." As an afterthought, she added, "Me and his attorney."

"Wow," Mike said, overwhelmed. "What luck. Have you seen the property? Where is it?"

"Just from the outside, and it's in Grove. I was there when you reached me."

"Well, I'm glad we *did* reach you. Seriously, your help has been great. It's practically solved the case; we'll just have to find him now."

She picked up her purse, and he escorted her out of the office. She asked, "So am I free to go look over my new house Monday?"

He answered her. "Yeah, just keep your cell phone handy."

They exited the building in the early evening. The air was still warm, and twilight was beginning to settle into night.

Emma turned to Mike as they stopped at her car. She held out her hand. "It was nice meeting you, Detective Mike Wells. I guess, call me if you need me."

He shook her hand warmly. "When we catch him, and I do mean *when* we will contact you as a witness." He frowned, his eyes concerned. "If you should feel scared or something out of the ordinary happens, please call me. I'll be there ASAP."

"Why should I feel scared?" Emma had no concerns now that she had talked to the police.

The detective glanced from the drawing to Emma. Mike looked at her as though he couldn't believe her naivety. He placed her hand between both of his, deadly serious. "Emma. Joseph Malone *does not* like witnesses. Before now, we had no proof he killed anyone. He *is* an evil man. Don't take him lightly. If Malone thinks you've talked to the police, and he knows who you are, he may come after you. If he does, we'll protect you."

He dropped her hand. "Go to Grove. Don't tell anyone where you're going. Keep your cell phone handy and put my number on speed dial."

"Right. Okay. Yes." Like an automaton, Emma took out her keys and unlocked her car. *What a dufus I am*! She had completely forgotten her fear when she thought the killer was chasing her. Now, it came back in full force as she slid behind the wheel.

She put the keys in the ignition and started the car. Mike tapped on her window, and she rolled it down.

"If you even have a feeling that something isn't right, call me."

Emma relaxed and smiled at his worried frown. "Yes, I will. I'll be fine." As an afterthought, giving him what she hoped was a flirtatious look, she smiled again. "I may just call you anyway." Before he could respond, she slipped the car into reverse to drive home.

Chapter Nine

Sunday was a lazy day for Emma. Mike told her not to tell anyone where she was going, but keeping her plans from her parents was impossible. Besides, they already knew a good portion of it since the detectives arrived on their doorstep.

She had brunch at their house and filled them in, finishing with the story of her unexpected inheritance. They both promised absolute secrecy, at least until Joseph Malone was caught and behind bars.

"But it'll be hard," her mother told her. "You know your aunts and uncles will be upset that we didn't tell them right away." She paused and added, "And your grandmother will feel insulted you didn't tell her. Not to mention Lyn, since you went in the jewelry store to shop for a present for Cassie." Lyn was Emma's older sister, whose daughter Cassie was the intended recipient of the birthstone jewelry that was never purchased.

"As soon as this is under control, they can all be told." She looked thoughtful. "Maybe I'll even have a big party at my new house. Yeah. I like that idea."

She sat at the breakfast nook table, the usual lemon-lime soda in her hand. "It's just that the detective made Joseph Malone sound pretty vengeful, and I think if we kept everyone out of the loop about me and my whereabouts and what I saw, we would all be safer."

"That makes sense," her dad agreed. "But it all

makes me think of a plot out of a movie, something that doesn't happen in real life."

"I know. But for right now, I'm going to take it a step at a time. I'll go to Grove tomorrow, sign papers, and take it from there." She stood and gave her parents each a quick hug. "I'll call you and let you know what's going on."

Back at her little apartment, she wandered about, uneasy. She went to the balcony and looked out, watching for any strangers lurking about or nondescript dark sedans. She didn't see any, but bland four-door cars seemed in plentiful supply. She never noticed before, but her neighbors did not have the best, newer models of transportation.

She packed a light bag on the chance she could spend the night in her new residence. Although she wasn't sure she wanted to do that alone.

She dozed on the couch and absent-mindedly rubbed Marms on the head. His long length was stretched out against her, and he purred in feline contentment. She hadn't decided what she should tell her employer tomorrow. If he wouldn't let her off, well, she would go anyway. Mr. Johnson had said she didn't need a job.

The theme song from a popular sitcom blasted across the room and jarred her awake. Tina called. Emma struggled up and around Marms. He opened one eye, saw no food was going to be involved, and curled back to sleep. Emma caught the phone just before it went to voicemail.

Tina was still distraught over her latest breakup. Erick had not returned any of her calls, and she hadn't been able to talk to him all weekend. This after he told her they were no longer compatible. He had taken his things and moved out.

"I just don't know what I'm going to do. I'm so lost without him," Tina wailed in Emma's ear. Emma imagined she had been crying since their girl's night.

"Why don't you come over here?" she suggested. "We'll talk, have some popcorn and soda, plot some horrible revenge." She looked over at Marms, snoring gently as he took up the center of the couch. "Marms and I could use some company."

"Oh, I don't know. Okay." Tina sniffed. "It's better than being here alone."

"Good. We'll see you in a little bit." Emma clicked off the phone and turned to Marms. "Well, sleepyhead, your rest is about to be disturbed. Tina's coming over, and she's sobbing over Erick." When Tina was upset and Marms was around, she tended to hold the big tomcat and rub him and hug him until he squirmed away and sought refuge behind the sofa. As though he understood, he opened his eyes wide and gave a long leisurely stretch, yawning and showing his sharp little teeth.

Emma went to the kitchen. To Marms, Emma in the kitchen meant food, so he jumped off the couch and followed her. She poured him some dinner, and he dove in.

It wasn't long before Tina knocked at her door. *She must have been ready to walk out when she called.* Emma opened the door to her friend. Tina stood hunched, her eyes red from crying, purse on one arm, and a backpack hanging off her shoulder.

"You spending the night?" Emma asked as Tina trudged into the room. Although she didn't care, Emma didn't remember that being part of the conversation.

"You don't mind, do you?" Tina slung the backpack

and purse onto the couch, then turned to face Emma as she closed the door. "I really don't want to be alone in the apartment, and I figured you wouldn't mind."

"No, of course not." Emma gave her a big hug. "You don't look so good. Have you been crying all weekend?" Tina's short blonde hair normally looked sleek and shiny and always hung perfectly around her face, a look Emma envied. Now, it was dull and lifeless.

Tina had a classic blonde look, with blue eyes and fair skin. The two girls were direct opposites. Tina was as short as Emma was tall, petite, although slightly rounded at five-foot-two, while her friend had a five-foot-eight slender stature. Both envied different attributes of the other.

"Want a soda or tea? Maybe a glass of wine?" Emma asked as she headed to the kitchen. Her friend trailed behind her. Tina pulled up on a barstool and looked at the young woman she considered her best friend.

"I think wine would be nice, and speaking of not looking so good, you don't either. Anything going on with you?"

"Actually, there is," Emma replied as she unscrewed the cap off an inexpensive bottle of wine. She knew Tina was upset and wanted to spend the afternoon whining and crying about Erick. Upon seeing her friend, Emma decided she would convince Tina to go to Grove with her. She didn't want to face this challenge and new circumstances all on her own. Tina was the perfect best friend to come along with her.

An elementary teacher, Tina had taught for one year when the school let her go due to cutbacks. She was scraping along as a substitute teacher and was in the perfect circumstances to drop everything and go to

Grove. The only thing that held her to Tulsa was Erick, and it sounded like he was out of the picture now, too.

They sat on the ends of the couch and faced each other as they sipped their wine. Emma told Tina all about what happened Thursday afternoon with the robbery and concluded with her interview with the police. She placed a box of tissues on the sofa in front of Tina should she have a momentary setback and begin to cry about Erick again.

Tina didn't have any setbacks. Emma's story of the robbery, murder, and inheritance so engrossed her friend that she forgot all about Erick and how he wronged her.

"So," Emma concluded, "I think you should come to Grove with me. I need someone to make sure I'm not doing something really stupid and help me understand everything that is going on." At Tina's raised eyebrows, Emma continued. "And it's perfect timing—you need to get away. Your job is iffy, and it will do Erick good for you to be out of pocket for a while." Emma had never told her friend, but she didn't care for this recent boyfriend. As far as she was concerned, she'd be happy if he was totally out of her friend's life.

"I promised Mike, the detective, that I wouldn't talk about the murder and all that, as he didn't want anyone knowing where I was. *But*, if you're with me, I think that hardly counts as telling anyone." She beamed at her friend, this little bit of logic making perfect sense to her.

Tina frowned. "You realize you are skewing the bit about not telling anyone, so you can get your own way, don't you?"

Emma nodded. "I know. But this feels right." She looked at Tina, imploring. "Please come."

Tina considered. "Okay." She smiled, her first since

arriving at the apartment. "How could I resist what sounds like an adventure? New town, new beginnings, an inheritance? Why not? Sure!"

"Woo hoo!" Emma jumped up and sat down her empty wine glass. She hugged her friend tightly. "Having you there will make this so much fun!"

"And you're sure about this? You were willed this estate?" Tina was still doubtful.

"Mr. Johnson was emphatic. And he said I could call him anytime, and I intend to call him first thing in the morning before I go to work. Just to make sure before I say anything to my boss about leaving."

"All right." Tina held out her empty wineglass. "Well, fill me up again and tell me all about this house and everything. I want to know all about it before I even get there."

Emma smiled broadly and took their glasses to the kitchen for refills. "I think I'll order a pizza. Pepperoni and extra cheese, okay?"

****

The girls spent the rest of the afternoon making plans around their upcoming trip to Grove. They decided to only stay overnight, as they didn't know what to expect with Emma's job—would they let her go right away? And if they didn't, did she want to push the issue and leave without notice?

Tina decided there was enough packed in her backpack, so she didn't need to go back to her apartment. "What about Marms?" She sat cross-legged on the couch, the big yellow cat curled asleep in her lap.

"He'll be okay for one day and night. And it's not like it's a long trip, just a couple of hours. I'll put plenty of food and water out for him and make sure his box is clean." She looked at the big feline curled in her friend's lap. He squinted at her as he dozed off. "He'll sulk a little at being left alone, but he'll get over it."

At ten o'clock, they were both exhausted and ready to call it a day. Tina turned to the news as she made a bed on the couch. She wondered if there would be any mention of the murder her friend witnessed. She figured it was old news now, but with Emma giving her fresh details, she wanted to listen while she got her bed arranged. Emma walked into the room to wish her friend a good night. A photo of Joseph Malone flashed up on the screen alongside the news anchor. Emma gasped. Her friend glanced at her and then turned her eyes to the screen also.

"Police are now looking for Joseph Malone, suspect in the murder of Sun's Jewelry Store owner, Jin Sin Sun. Identified by a witness to the murder, Mr. Malone is considered armed and dangerous. If you have any knowledge of Mr. Malone's whereabouts, please do not approach him. Please call Crimestoppers at …"

"Oh my gosh." Emma didn't hear the rest of the sentence. "Oh, dear. Now he knows for sure." She sat on Tina's tightly stretched blanket.

Tina looked at her friend. "What am I missing? Who knows what?"

"Joseph Malone. Now he knows for sure there is a witness, and he knows I've talked to the police. If he doesn't know who I am, it won't be long before he does. If the detective is right, he'll come looking for me." She looked at Tina, her tone sober and her face filled with worry. "I'm sorry, I can't ask you to come with me now. It's too dangerous."

"Nonsense." The teacher in Tina surfaced. "Right

now, you need someone with you, and you're not talking me out of it. I'm going. Now, get off my bed." She waved her hand at Emma to make her move so Tina could lie down for the night. As Emma rose, her cell phone blared. There was no distinctive ring, and she didn't recognize the incoming number.

"Hello?" Hesitant, she answered, her tone lowered. Tina looked at her, eyebrow skewed in a you're kidding look.

"Miss Stone? This is Detective Mike Wells."

Her voice returned to normal. "Oh, hi. Wasn't expecting you. Didn't know who was calling…"

"Well, whatever you were doing to your voice didn't work."

"Sudden impulse. Probably shouldn't have answered at all, huh?" Emma thought her fake voice was more productive than that.

"Answering was the right thing to do, as your phone probably has your name in the voicemail, doesn't it? So, whoever's calling knows they've found you right away." He sounded sure in his theory. "Have you seen the news?"

"Yeah. I didn't think you wanted it known there was a witness."

"We didn't. Just wanted Malone's picture put on the air. But it's too late now. How are you doing?" Concern came through the phone line to her.

"Okay." *Deep breath, Emma, talk to him.* "So if he hasn't already figured out that I saw him, which, since he chased me on foot, apparently, he knew, now he knows I've talked to the police. All he must do, if he hasn't already done so, is figure out who I am so he can find me and kill me. Probably in some hideous, torturous way."

"Glad you're taking this so well, but you're right." He chuckled, then coughed to cover it. "We think you should go ahead and get out of town, maybe earlier than planned."

"I am leaving tomorrow, maybe in the afternoon, because of my job."

"Go in the morning, forget the job. I'll talk to the law firm. You need to get on the move. I'll have a police unit circle your apartment complex tonight."

"That would be nice, but surely, he couldn't find me that fast? I mean, we've figured he didn't think I went to the police, so has he even been looking for me?" Emma just refused to believe she could be in danger so quickly.

"He's extraordinarily careful about details, and you are a detail. Even if he believed you didn't talk, I'm sure he's been searching to find your identity."

"Okay, send a policeman to check on me if you want. And we'll scoot out of here first thing in the morning."

"We?"

"My friend Tina's going to Grove with me." At his startled exclamation, she continued, "We've discussed this all afternoon, Tina and I, and it's decided. She knows she's in danger." She looked at Tina, eyes wider than normal, her brow creased in worry. "And Marms, too. We were going to leave him behind for a day, but we'll all go."

"And who is Marms?"

"My cat. He's very protective of me."

He let out a long sigh. "Very well. I'll call the unit to make some extra runs. Do you have security at that apartment complex?"

She snorted. "Yeah, supposedly."

"I'll call them, too." He added, "All right, call me when you leave, okay?"

With a slight smile, she agreed. "All right. Why?"

"So, I know you're okay."

"Oh." A pleasant little tingle crept over her.

"It's my job. I need to make sure you're safe."

"Oh." The tingle evaporated. It was his job.

She sighed. "I'll call you in the morning." Emma hung up before he could say anything further.

She looked at Tina, her eyes full of questions. "*Detective* Wells wants to make sure I'm safe, so I have to call him in the morning when we leave."

Chapter Ten

It was six a.m. Monday morning. Both girls were preparing for their road trip. Tina'd showered first and stood at the kitchen counter. She arranged her makeup while Emma bathed.

Marms glowered at Tina from under the coffee table. He'd seen Emma bring out his cat carrier late last night. That was never a good thing.

Since it had been late when they changed their plans to go to Grove and stay longer, they decided to wait until this morning and go by Tina's apartment for more of her necessities. She finished her makeup and popped a few things into the backpack. She placed it beside the door, ready to pick it up when they left.

There was a noise outside. Tina stopped and listened. She stood on tiptoes, looked through the eyehole, and gasped. There was a man outside the door. He was just standing there, leaning against the wall, but obviously waiting for them.

Tina backed away and shook her hands in agitation. She had to tell Emma, maybe she should call that detective, or the police, or someone.

"Emma!" Tina whisper-screamed as she ran to the bathroom and pounded on the door. "Emma, there's a man outside!"

Wrapped in a faded beach towel, Emma emerged, a terry cloth turban around her hair. "What?"

"There's a man outside your door! He's just standing there, waiting!" She shoved her cell phone at her friend. "I think you should call 911."

"Let me look first, then we'll panic. Keep your phone." Emma padded barefoot, clad in her towel, and squinted through the eyehole. She heaved a sigh of relief.

"I don't know what he's doing here, but it's Detective Wells."

She opened the door a crack to peek out and saw him jerk upright. "Good morning, Detective. What are you doing here?"

He could see one eye and side of her face. Obviously, she just walked out of the shower. "I wanted to make sure you were okay and got on your way all right. I was going to trail behind you out of town, make sure you weren't followed."

Emma thought he was overdoing it but felt relieved at his presence. "Okay. Give us a minute."

She shut the door and turned back to Tina. "I'll get dressed. You let him in and see if he wants some coffee or something. Just let me get my things."

"What about getting my stuff?"

Emma thought. "As you're making him coffee, tell him we're going to go by your place, and if he wants, he can tag along." She smiled. "He might be useful in carrying a few bags."

She turned and strolled back to the bedroom, re-emerged with jeans, underwear, and T-shirt slung over her arm. She entered the bathroom, and Tina returned to the door.

She looked out again through the eyehole. She had to make sure no bad men had overcome the detective. He was still alone, patiently leaning against the wall. She opened the door.

"Would you like to come in? I was just making some coffee." Tina smiled, and he smiled back.

"I don't mind waiting out here. I'm not here to impose or cause any problems."

"No problem at all. Come on in and have a seat. Emma's getting dressed. We're almost ready."

He walked in and followed her to the tiny kitchen. The coffee was dripping through the basket, filling the small pot below. She smiled at the detective as he perched on one of the counter stools. She stuck out her hand. "I'm Tina."

He shook her hand. "Glad to meet you, Tina. Mike Wells. Detective, Tulsa P.D." As she gathered three coffee cups, cream, and sugar, he said, "So you're going with Emma to Grove. What has she told you?"

"Oh, everything. We talked most of the night. Emma was startled to hear a witness described on the news. I think she was surprised they even mentioned the murder. We were thinking it was old news now." Tina pulled out some spoons. "Cream or sugar?"

"Black, thanks. We're not sure how they latched onto the knowledge there was a witness. The chief had given the order to have them put Malone's picture on the news so the public would be aware and on the lookout for him." He watched the coffee dripping into the pot. "He's not happy about it, and neither am I."

The coffee finished, and Tina poured them both a cup. As he waited for his to cool, Mike commented, "We never wanted a witness mentioned, didn't want Emma in danger. We were just glad to *have* a witness."

Tina added sugar to her coffee and stirred it slowly. She looked at the detective, her eyes serious. "This last week has been hard on Emma. She's pretty sensitive, and although she puts up a hard front, she's a soft touch. Being in the middle of the robbery, seeing Mr. Sun dead, nothing like this has ever happened in her whole *life*, let alone in just a few days. I think it's a bit overwhelming, but she's handling it really well."

Mike asked, "And you're telling me this, why?"

"Just so you'll know." She put down her coffee, her eyes still serious. "Emma doesn't look it, but she's tough. She'll hang in there for whatever needs to be done, testifying, facing up to the monster that killed Mr. Sun, whatever it takes. But when it's over, she'll break down into quiet little pieces." She paused. "Then she'll be back, stronger and a little bit wiser." Tina took another sip. "I can't threaten you, you being police and all..." His eyebrows went up. "Please don't let her know I told you. I don't want you to think she's weak. She's not." Her eyes were serious over the rim of her cup.

"Well." He sat up straighter, and they both glanced at the bathroom door as the lock clicked prior to opening. "I'll keep that in mind. Thank you."

"Welcome. By the way, I was supposed to tell you that we're dropping by my apartment to get a few of my things on our way out. Do you want to follow us over there?"

"Of course."

They both turned as Emma emerged from the bathroom, her hair damp from the shower, a bag of cosmetics in one hand, blow dryer and brush in the other. She turned to the bedroom to pack away those items and returned with a fully-packed rolling carrier. She deposited the carrier by the door next to Tina's backpack. Tina poured her a cup of coffee.

"So, de-tec-tive, just making sure the culprits got out of town early this morning, huh?" Her eyes glittered as she remembered that he was *just doing his job* the night before. She blew on her hot coffee as she settled on a stool beside him. "As you can see, we are going."

"I'm just making sure you're still okay. And apparently, you are." His gaze took in her clean look and scent. Her freshly shampooed hair smelled slightly of soap mixed with a light perfume that reminded him of wildflowers. Her hair was not tied up as it had been Saturday but fell to her shoulders, wild around her face. Her T-shirt fit snugly and proclaimed her love for wildlife, while her jeans hugged her hips comfortably. Her feet were bare, toenails painted a shiny red.

"Tina tell you we still need to stop by her apartment?"

"Yeah, no problem." He jerked in his seat, and looked down at his right leg.

Marms decided he needed some attention from their visitor and was standing on his hind legs, his front paws reaching up and pawing at Mike's knee.

"Wow, that's some cat." He reached down to rub Marm's head and scratch behind his ears. Marms turned his head so Mike could reach the spot better and closed his eyes in bliss.

Tina chuckled, and Emma filled him in. "This is Marms, so named because he's a marmalade cat. As you can see, he's also a little on the big side. He'll eat just about anything, and he's not shy."

"So, I see. He's one of the biggest cats I think I've ever seen. What's he weigh?"

"About twenty pounds." Emma took a couple of big sips of her coffee, suddenly anxious to be on their way.

"Since he seems to like you, you want to put him in his carrier?" Emma pointed toward the carrier beside the couch.

Mike shot her a look of, *you think I can't?* and bent his head, talking gently to the big cat while he continued to rub his ears. He went over and sat on the couch, and Marms padded right after him. As soon as he was seated and patted his lap, the big tomcat jumped up and began to curl up. "Now don't get too comfortable, big fella, because you can't stay long."

Emma and Tina glanced at each other. Tina whispered, "Better him than us," remembering the last time they tried to get Marms in his carrier. He had fought them tooth and nail, resulting in a long scratch across Emma's left hand.

Emma stood and went to rinse out her cup. "I still have a few more things to get and will be right out." She disappeared into her bedroom, leaving Tina to watch Mike woo the cat.

He reached around the side of the couch and moved the carrier out in front of them, easily in view. Marms didn't pay any notice to the carrier. He continued to lap up the attention.

"Do you have an old towel to go in this for him, something Emma has used and not washed yet? And does he have a favorite toy, maybe something with catnip? And toss a few kibbles of food in there."

"Sure." Tina hurried to the bedroom, conferred with Emma, and grabbed a towel from a hook in the bathroom. "She used this yesterday."

He gently put it in the carrier, meanwhile still stroking the cat.

"Toy," Tina repeated as she scanned the living

room. There didn't seem to be any cat toys about.

Emma exited the bedroom at that time. Another fully-packed shoulder bag hung from her arm. Clutched in one hand was a green fuzzy round bug-like object with what appeared to be a hundred legs dangling from it. She waved it at Mike and dropped it in his hand as she went by the couch. "That's his favorite—he carries it around a lot. I think it has catnip in it."

"Great. Now, if one of you will hold the back of the carrier so it doesn't scoot."

Emma dropped her bags by the door. She sat delicately on the carrier to hold it in place.

Mike continued to talk to Marms as he got up, slipped the cat into the carrier face first, put the toy in with him, and locked the door. Then he stood. "There you go."

Marms let out one meow, and Mike leaned down to talk to him, wiggling his finger in through a window in the side. Marms rubbed his cheek against it. When Mike straightened, Marms circled and lay down.

Tina watched in amazement, then turned to her friend. "Emma, you need to keep him around. Marms has never been this well-behaved."

Emma glared at her, her back to Mike so he couldn't see her face. Tina beamed a bright smile, knowing full well she was teasing her friend and possibly making Mike uncomfortable. She didn't care.

"Are we ready to go?" Emma growled as she turned to the door, ready to pick up her things and hurl them down the steps. It irritated her that Marms was being so cooperative, Tina acted like Mike was part of the family, and Mike being whatever. It was annoying.

"Hold it." Mike beat her to the door. "Let me take a

couple of bags and go first. Can I have your keys?" Emma grabbed them off the counter and sullenly handed them to him. He picked up a couple of bags and headed out.

The minute he was gone, both friends turned on each other.

"Why are you being so friendly with him?"

"Why are you being so hateful? Emma, look at him. He's gorgeous! And you act like you want to beat him over the head with something! Even Marms likes him, and Marms doesn't like just anyone." Marms wasn't shy. He was quick to show his temper to anyone he didn't like or had earned his displeasure.

Tina looked at her friend, confused. "Is this because he says he is *doing his job* and you hope it's a little bit more than that?" At Emma's look that maybe her friend had hit the sore spot, Tina continued, "Then relax and take it for what it is. Who knows? Maybe it won't be just his job someday. But you can't treat him like you hate him and expect him to be nice to you all the time. I think he's being very patient with you." That said, her friend took a different tack.

"Besides, today is the first day of a big adventure. You have inherited an estate, money, and I'm thrilled because you've asked me to come along. I wish you would act a little bit excited, too. Please, lighten up."

Tina's beratement had some effect on Emma, and she realized she had been a little harsh. She tamped down her anger as she looked at her friend. "You're right. Besides, De-tec-tive Wells may be out of my life soon enough. I have a whole new life ahead of me, in a way." She leaned toward her friend and said, "I can't wait to see the inside of that house. It's got to be beautiful."

"This is going to be fun. I am so ready for this little road trip." Tina grinned at Emma.

"Me, too. Okay, let's get some coffee for the road and see if Mike will carry Marms down the stairs, too."

****

Emma helped Tina gather what else she would need for their stay while the detective kept an eye on the parking lot of her apartment. After much discussion, it was decided Tina should drive her own vehicle to Grove, following behind Emma, with Mike behind both for a short distance. The decision was made when Mike argued that Grove would be a much safer place for Tina's vehicle for a few days than Tulsa. And, of course, it gave Tina the freedom to move about without having to ask Emma for the keys to her car.

At about eight a.m., the three cars proceeded east out of Tulsa; Emma with her bags in the back and Marms doing the occasional pitiful meow from his carrier on the front seat. Tina followed in her car, and Mike brought up the rear.

As they reached Claremore, Mike gave Emma a call. "I think everything looks okay, Emma." He paused. "I'll stay in touch. But please, call me if you need *anything* or anything seems wrong, no matter how small it might seem."

At her polite answer, he was about to say goodbye when she asked, "Do you ever get a day off, detective?"

"Yeah." He chuckled. "We are allowed some free time. Why?" Surely, she wouldn't be so bold as to ask him out while he was working on her case.

"I thought you might like to come to Grove and see where I'll be living. You should see it because, after all, it's, like, part of all this. You need to know exactly where

I'll be." Emma figured it was against all kinds of protocol to ask the detective out, no matter how attracted to him she was, while he was associated with the case. But she was a witness after all, and he had stated that Malone would try to find her and kill her.

Tina's little chewing out had done her some good. She decided to be nicer to him, and if he said he couldn't, well, she would accept it.

"I'm off Saturday. Would that work?"

Emma released a silent breath, glad he accepted her invitation. She smiled as she answered. "That would work just fine. How about early afternoon? And stay for dinner?" She gave a little laugh, a rich throaty chuckle. "I'm not saying I would do the cooking, which you should be glad about. But supposedly, I have a housekeeper who also cooks, and I bet with a little bit of bribing, I could get her to cook on a Saturday."

"That sounds great, Emma. I'll look forward to seeing you then." He signed off after telling her to drive carefully and again advised her to contact him immediately if she felt anything was not right.

Chapter Eleven

As she drove the turnpike, Emma placed a phone call to Mr. Johnson. He was fine with her coming that morning. He had no set appointments and no problem with Tina being her guest. However, he cautioned her that they had several things to go over, including a visit to the local bank, so it might take longer than she anticipated before they could go to the house. Emma assured him it was fine. Since she worked for an attorney, she understood things often took longer than expected. Tina was along for the adventure, and she was patient.

Emma devoted her attention to the road. She relaxed, ready to sift through whatever paperwork necessary at the attorney's office, and looked forward to an exciting new turn in her life. Marms let out a worried yowl as a reminder to Emma he was still on the passenger seat.

"Ah, I know, fella. But this will be neat, you'll see. You'll have this great big house to roam in instead of a little apartment. You'll like it." She wiggled her finger through his air holes on the side, and he rubbed his face against it.

****

Around eleven a.m., they pulled into the attorney's parking lot. Emma carried Marms, telling the surprised receptionist that she really didn't want to leave him in the car. Tina took a seat in a plush chair in the corner of the reception area, and Emma sat the carrier beside her. The cat let out a plaintive meow. Tina leaned forward and talked to him while Emma gave her name, stating Mr. Johnson was expecting her.

The attorney came out of his office, all smiles. He shook Emma's hand, and she introduced Tina, whom he greeted warmly. His gaze fell to the large pet carrier, where another yowl erupted.

Emma waved a hand at the carrier. "This is Marms. I really needed to bring him along, too. Hope you don't mind."

"No, of course not." He indicated his office toward the back. "Please come in, and let's get down to business." Emma followed him into his office, and he shut the door.

****

Tina had brought a book with her, as she knew she had to wait while Emma attended to legalities. She sat down to read. A half hour passed. She put down the book and rolled her stiff shoulders. She stood and walked over to the receptionist.

"Do you have a vending machine? Like for a soda?"

"No, but we keep sodas in the refrigerator for clients. What would you like?"

"A cola would be great."

"Be right back." The receptionist rose and went toward a back room.

Tina wandered around the small reception area, doing little stretches to ease her stiff muscles. She saw the local paper on an end table, picked it up, and shook it open. *Might as well read up on what the locals are doing.*

At the bottom of the front page, a headline jumped out at her: *YOUNG WOMAN INHERITS ESTATE.*

"Uh oh." Tina was totally absorbed in the story when the receptionist returned and handed her a cold cola.

"Thank you." She mumbled as she took the soda and continued to read the article. They had Emma's name and everything in the story. Of course, they had nothing about Emma witnessing the robbery, for which she was greatly relieved.

It was the morning paper. She addressed the receptionist again. "Did you see this article?"

The receptionist looked at the headline. "No, but I don't read the local paper very often. Why?"

"Just wondering. Don't suppose you would know where they would get their information."

"No clue." She turned back to her computer screen and resumed her work.

Tina sat down, folded the paper, and held it, maybe a bit too tightly.

Marms was restless and let out another loud yowl. "I know, Marms. It won't be long, and we can let you out." She looked again at the paper and glanced back to the door where Mr. Johnson and Emma disappeared.

"I don't know about this," she muttered, "but somehow, I don't think it's a good thing to have her name plastered all over the newspaper. And everyone knowing she has inherited this…" She thought of lottery winners who suddenly had relatives and people pop out of the woodwork. She glanced down as the carrier wobbled when Marms shifted his position. "I hope that doesn't happen to Emma, Marms."

Another half hour went by, and Emma and Mr.

Johnson emerged from the office. Emma's eyes were glazed, but overall, she looked happy. Tina stood as Emma approached, and Mr. Johnson advised the receptionist he would be out for a couple of hours.

"Look!" Tina held the paper in front of Emma and directed her gaze to the headline. "You are on the front page of the paper!" Emma scanned the article as Tina impatiently hovered around her.

Mr. Johnson finished giving instructions to his receptionist and turned to them. "Is something wrong?"

Emma showed Mr. Johnson the paper. "How did they get this information about me? And what's going to happen now?"

Mr. Johnson glanced over the article. "I don't know how they got your information, but I don't think there's anything to worry about. If you need it, there's good security at the house, and the police here are quick to respond." He turned toward the door.

"Does he know that you witnessed, you know?" Tina whispered to her friend.

"No," Emma answered softly, then plastered a smile on her face for Mr. Johnson, who held the door for her. She reached down and picked up Marms. Mr. Johnson, noting how heavy the cat carrier seemed to be, took it from her.

"Here, I'll take him." He carried Marms to Emma's car, and Emma and Tina followed behind. They got in their respective cars and followed Mr. Johnson down the street to the bank.

****

Emma signed all the necessary documents, and Mr. Johnson and the manager both gave her instructions. Finally, she was able to leave, some money in her pocket and new checks ordered with her name on them. Mr. Johnson gave the bank manager her address, so a debit and credit card could be sent to her. Emma looked at the address on one of the documents. She hadn't even known her address yet.

Tina and Marms waited patiently. The air was cool, and they had parked in the shade.

As Emma and Mr. Johnson walked out of the bank, Mr. Johnson smiled a big smile. "Now," he said, "the fun part. Let's go see your estate."

Emma relaxed. The paperwork, the drudge part, was over, at least for the time being. She grinned at Tina and gave her a thumbs-up sign. As she walked to her car, she called to her friend, "Just follow us!" She slid in and started her car.

Tina did the same. Their small caravan drove slowly out of town and over the bridge. At a slight hill, Mr. Johnson signaled to turn left, and both Emma and Tina signaled to do the same.

The driveway was long and winding. Then, the final long sweep of the lane, the towering trees, and the house were before them. It was as beautiful as Emma remembered. She pulled her car behind Mr. Johnson, stopped and shut off her engine, then gazed at the house. She heard Tina ease behind her and park. Emma opened her door and stood, staring at the towering residence.

How can it be possible this belongs to me? All the money talk they had just finished, some of it confusing, and now this house. Her gaze roamed from side to side slowly, absorbing the proud lines and graceful sweep of the entrance, three stories rising tall. The breeze in the trees softly whispered, and Emma felt they were welcoming her home.

****

Marms's loud wail startled Emma out of her reverie. Mr. Johnson walked to the front door, key in hand, ready to unlock it for her. Emma hurried around the car, opened the passenger door, and pulled the cat carrier onto the sidewalk.

Tina let out a breath as she walked up behind her. "Wow. Somehow, I didn't think it would be like this." She followed her friend up the steps where the attorney waited.

The entrance was a round turret built against the straight lines of the rest of the house. Double doors were set within the wall, and the lawyer turned the key. He pushed the doors inward, then stood back and waited. "Welcome home."

Emma and Tina stepped through the entrance doors, both girls looking around. The large entry opened to a central white marble staircase that rose to the second story and then spread to the left and right for a wide landing. At the ceiling, a sparkling chandelier dominated. On each side of the foyer were twin doors, and Emma could hardly contain her curiosity as to where they led.

The sound of Mr. Johnson putting the carrier down caught their attention. "Where would you like Mr. Marms?" he asked. "I think he's ready to get out of this box." Another loud yowl confirmed his suspicion.

"Oh, yes. Just a minute." Emma ran back to her car and retrieved a bag of litter and a new litter box. A small bag of cat food was under the other arm.

Coming back alongside the lawyer with her arms full of kitty supplies, she realized she didn't have a clue where to go with it. "Where do you suggest?"

"There's a utility room that would suffice for now if you agree." At Emma's nod, the attorney led both girls to the rear of the house, past several doorways, and into a large, cheery laundry room.

Mr. Johnson set the carrier on the floor and closed another connecting door. Tina took the litter from Emma and started pouring it into the box while Emma opened the carrier door to release the noisy feline.

For being so verbal, Marms took his time getting out of the carrier. When he finally strolled out, all eyes were on him. Emma rubbed his head, and he nudged against her hand, then began to investigate his fresh territory.

"Are you ready to get a real look at the rest of the house?" Mr. Johnson asked. At their mutual nod, the attorney led them from the utility area through the kitchen and the adjoining rooms. The girls followed like puppies. Occasionally, Emma would ask a question that would involve a detailed answer, but mostly, she contained her curiosity. Tina kept silent except for a brief exclamation now and then.

In the living room, they paused before re-entering the foyer. The room had two sofas and several chairs scattered about for comfortable, cozy seating. The dining room they had passed through held a huge table with twelve chairs and at least two sideboards. Emma was curious. This was a home for entertainment, decorated with exceptional taste. Why would he shut himself away? She voiced her thoughts.

"I understand why you would question that," the lawyer answered. "When Mrs. Kerwood was alive, there was laughter, food, drinks, frequent times with friends around. It was after she passed that Mr. Kerwood became a recluse. She died around seven years ago." A sad smile crossed his face.

"The dining room has been unused. The last couple of years of his life, he either ate in his room, which originally was the den, or at the kitchen table. He and the O'Malleys got along well."

"How long have the O'Malleys been with him?"

"A long time, and Ms. Karroll, his nurse, has been with him for at least five years. He took care of them well, financially, so they aren't to be pitied by any means."

"Oh, I wasn't pitying them, but just wondered why he would leave all this to a stranger when he had good people that cared for him." Emma didn't understand Mr. Kerwood's reasoning.

"I can't explain it. He outlived all his friends, family, and he had no desire to sell or give away his possessions. He decided he'd just keep it all, and whoever inherited his estate could deal with it as they wanted. There were certain things Mr. Kerwood didn't confide in me, and that was one of them. I asked him one time why he didn't leave this to the O'Malleys, or Ms. Karroll, and he simply said, 'Because I don't want to.' If I persisted, he'd get upset. I didn't want to anger him, so I let it drop."

****

Turning the doorknob to return to the foyer, he led them across to the matching doors on the other side.

"On this side of the house is the library, the den, and the downstairs bathroom. The den is where Mr. Kerwood spent most of his remaining years. As I indicated earlier, he had it converted to a bedroom, so he didn't have to climb the stairs."

Mr. Johnson opened the door and flipped a switch.

Light flooded the room. "This is the library," he announced.

There was a scent in the room any book lover would recognize. Books. Hundreds of books. Three of the four walls were lined with shelves, all packed with a variety of reading materials. Two windows allowed natural light to come streaming in.

Other than the tomes, a heavy mahogany desk dominated the opposite corner from the door. The desk was clear of clutter, a well-padded roller chair positioned in place under it. By all appearances, the office was ready for someone to sit and begin a day of paperwork.

Two tall shelves of books stood against the wall behind the desk, and between them was a bronze motif. A folksy piece of art, it attracted Tina. As her friend studied it, Emma wandered over to gaze also. "Kind of an odd piece of art," she commented.

"Not normally my style," Tina said. "But there's something about it I like."

The motif was two feet wide and square. A large, straggly tree devoid of leaves covered the center, with a solitary bench under it. The sky on the left showed the sun, recessed into the metal, with rays springing outward, while the sky to the right displayed a quarter moon. The tree, moon, and bench were overlaid onto the background.

"It makes me feel lonely," Emma declared. At the door on the other side of the room, she asked Mr. Johnson where it led.

"That's Mr. Kerwood's bedroom."

Jerking her hand away, she asked. "He died in here?"

"He did. Peacefully, in his sleep."

Emma glanced over to see Tina watching her. Suddenly, she regretted her curiosity at Mr. Kerwood's reasons for leaving the house and money to a stranger. Was this room, where he spent the final years of his life, going to reveal just how strange his mind had turned? Was it going to be a pit of filth, piles of newspapers lining the walls, bags of trash waiting to be thrown out, uneaten food growing mold? *No sense putting it off.* She turned the knob and entered the room, Tina a few steps behind her.

Chapter Twelve

Emma breathed a sigh of relief. There were no bags of trash or uneaten food. The room was sparsely decorated, with a queen-size bed, bedside table, and a chest of drawers. A lamp sat by the bedside. A framed photo and a book lay on the table. The photo displayed a man and woman leaning against a rock wall in the country. The man had his arm about the woman, and she leaned back against him. Both smiled at the camera. *This must be the Kerwoods when they were young.* Emma's heart grew warm when she realized the picture set where he would see it as he went to sleep at night.

On the other side of the room was a recliner, upholstered in a red and black plaid. Obviously, a favorite piece of furniture as it was well-worn and listed a little to the left. Across from both the bed and the chair was a large-screen TV. Its remote rested on the arm of the recliner. A full-length closet dominated the other wall.

Emma was a little uncomfortable. So far, the rest of the house appeared like a model home; clean, uncluttered, and few personal items around. This room was different. Besides the picture and the recliner that would have looked out of place in the rest of the house, there was a real sense that somebody lived there.

"What am I supposed to do with his things? You know, his clothes, his *stuff.*"

"That's up to you. It's all yours now." At Emma's dazed expression, Mr. Johnson added, "There is a good thrift store in town, and they are always looking for donations. I'm sure they'd be happy to take whatever you'd give them. And Mr. Kerwood would approve."

"Okay, good, that's good," Emma murmured. So far, it had been an adventure, inheriting a big house in a beautiful setting, nice furniture, well kept. But seeing where Mr. Kerwood had spent time brought it all home that it had belonged to a real person who had spent many years of his life here and now was dead. Emma raised her hands in the air in a defensive posture and turned to the doorway. "I'm sorry. I need some air."

As she passed the attorney, Emma commented, "I don't know about Tina, but I think I'd like to bring our stuff in, do a little unpacking, and check out one of the local restaurants in town."

"We've got a fine Mexican restaurant out by the Sailboat Bridge. If you like Mexican, it's my treat."

Emma nodded, accepting without asking Tina. She knew her friend would eat Mexican every day of the week if she could.

As they walked out of the house, Emma turned to lock the front door for the first time. She paused to run her hand along the fine old wood, gently stroking the graceful handle. Hearing the doors slam and the engine start jerked her to attention. She turned to run down the steps. She slid into the seat as Mr. Johnson pulled out of the driveway and drove toward town.

****

Conversation was casual and comfortable as the three sat around a table in the quiet restaurant. It was midafternoon, and business was slow, but the food was delicious. Emma picked at her food, planning on taking a snack box home with her, while Tina scarfed down her dinner with extra enchilada sauce.

Mr. Johnson encouraged them to explore the town, stating that it might be a bit on the small side compared to Tulsa, but the natives were friendly, and there were ample shopping opportunities.

"Oh, and before I forget, Mrs. O'Malley is very anxious to meet you. She'll probably be knocking on your door first thing in the morning." He took a sip of his water. "Or, she may be cooking breakfast for you, and the wonderful smell will waft you right out of your beds."

"Does she have a key?" City slicker Emma worried at how many people had keys to her new home.

"She's not supposed to have, and don't be worried about her bothering you. She has better manners than that. Mr. O'Malley is also anxious to meet you, but he is more, um, subdued than his missus." He scooped up the last of his rice. "As I said before, they both want to stay on the estate, doing what they have been doing all these years, and I think you ought to consider it. Mrs. O'Malley is a wonderful cook and housekeeper, and the grounds are quite a handful. Mr. O'Malley does an exceptional job keeping them looking as good as they do."

Emma signaled the waiter over and asked for a take-home box. She turned to Mr. Johnson. "I guess this seems like a silly question, but I have enough to pay them, right?"

Mr. Johnson nodded as he smiled. "Yes, you have plenty. Were you listening this morning as we went over the assets in my office?"

117

"Yes, but I don't think it sank in." Confused, she looked back and forth from Tina to Mr. Johnson. "What am *I* supposed to do? I'm not used to being idle and just sitting around. I've always either gone to school, had a part-time or a full-time job. Sometimes all the above." Tina didn't offer any helpful suggestions, so Emma turned her attention back to the attorney.

Mr. Johnson said, "If I were you, I would take some time to just be idle. Look around at what you've inherited, think about what you'd like to do, want to do with your life, but take your time. There's no reason to rush into anything. Maybe do some volunteer work to keep busy." He leaned forward to stress his meaning. "You have an opportunity few people get, with enough money to truly do what makes you happy. So take some time to learn what is in your heart." He leaned back as the waiter arrived with Emma's box and the check. He dug out his wallet, handed his credit card to the waiter as he said to Emma, "I mean it. *Relax.*"

The waiter came back with the final receipt. Mr. Johnson added his signature and a tip. Emma placed her lunch leftovers in the box for a late-night snack. It was time to return to her new home.

****

The attorney helped carry their luggage up to the second level. At the landing, he'd motioned to the right, stating that was originally the master bedroom, although both were basically the same rooms, with sitting rooms and private baths. There were four other bedrooms on the same floor, with a central bath. The stairway to the third floor was at the back of the house.

He turned to leave after he described the layout, and Emma walked to the front door with him, thanking him again for all his time and help.

"It has been my pleasure." He shook Emma's hand, pleased with the new owner of the estate. "Enjoy yourselves and call me if you need anything. Feel free to use the cell number, day or night."

"Thank you." Emma smiled and watched as he left. She hurried up the stairs where Tina waited, her eyes bright with curiosity, ready to see the rest of the house.

This time Emma didn't hesitate but turned the knob to the first bedroom and pushed the door open. A king-size bed stood against the wall, situated between windows. It boasted a large solid frame, the headboard standing about six feet high, rising toward a twelve-foot ceiling. At each corner of the footboard was a thin but sturdy post. On one wall were two doors, and Emma walked to the nearest while Tina went to the other. They exchanged looks, then both opened one. Tina had a large walk-in closet filled with women's clothes and shoes. Emma apparently had Mr. Kerwood's. They whipped the doors shut as smells of musty air and long unused clothing hit them.

"That can wait until I call the thrift store, don't you think?" Emma asked.

Tina nodded. Next, they inspected Tina's bedroom. It was essentially the same. In one closet, they found the necessary bedding to set up the beds for the night.

Sighing, Emma stated, "I'm tired. After making our beds, do you want to fool with putting our stuff up?"

Tina looked as tired as Emma. "I think I'll drag out what I need for the night, worry with the rest later."

"Sounds good. I'm going to get Marms, bring him up for the night."

"Okay." Tina picked through the bags as Emma

thumped down the stairs.

"*Meroww.*" Marms sat on top of the dryer, paws curled in front of him, gaze already locked on Emma.

"I didn't forget you. This seemed like the best place for you for a while."

Emma rubbed his big head before she pulled him off the appliance. Previously, Tina had left him a bowl of water and some food. By all appearances, he had devoured it.

The thought came to Emma that she needed to check the doors and make sure everything was locked tight. So many other things had been discussed that day she had totally forgotten that there might still be a killer looking for her. Scary how snug and complacent she already felt in her new surroundings.

Emma checked the front door, which was unlocked. With Marms trailing behind, she next inspected the laundry room door that led outside, which was still locked, and finally, the patio door. Emma stepped outside and shut the door before Marms could slip through. For the moment, she wanted to satisfy her curiosity.

They were so busy getting acquainted with the interior Emma hadn't looked around outdoors. Now was a quiet time. Through the dusky evening, she could identify dwellings where she assumed the O'Malleys and the nurse lived.

The three houses sat at a slight elevation, a comfortable walking distance from the primary abode. Mature trees separated them, providing privacy and shade. Well-worn stone paths led from each house toward the main residence. The O'Malleys only had to step out their back door and walk a short distance to the mansion. Lights came on in one of them, and as Emma watched, a second light came on, apparently in an adjoining room. She assumed that must be the home of the O'Malleys.

The air had turned cooler. Sitting on a patio glider, Emma drew her legs up, wrapped her arms around her knees, and looked at the night sky. The air was clear, and the stars sparkled with a brightness she never saw in the city. The drone of a semi on the highway far below echoed up to her. An occasional hardy cricket, reluctant to give up the summer, chirped in the darkness. Otherwise, the night was quiet. Emma sent up a little prayer of thankfulness.

She turned to go in and stooped down to prevent Marms from escaping. Emma locked the door and turned out the light, encouraging the feisty feline to follow her. At the bedroom, Marms trotted beside her, leaped on the bed, and flopped down to watch her. She rubbed his head. Once. When he discovered that was all he was going to get, he began his cleaning routine while Emma prepared for bed.

Emma slipped under the covers and turned out the light. Marms moved alongside, curling next to her, and they slept.

Chapter Thirteen

Doorbell chimes jerked Emma awake. Groggy with sleep, she struggled to sit and recognize her surroundings. When she did, she fell back against the pillow, exhausted. She had not slept well. Strange noises creaked and groaned throughout the night, and Emma didn't feel comfortable enough in her new home to explore their origins. Her thoughts had rambled, reminding her why she was here. Joseph Malone murdered Mr. Sun. Although her body was exhausted, it was after four in the morning before she slept. The doorbell. What if Malone had found her?

Wait. Malone wouldn't ring the doorbell.

Chimes rang again. Tina opened Emma's door and peered in; tousled hair fell over her face as she tied her robe. "Did you hear that? Some idiot is at the door! It's only…" She squinted at her watch. "Eight o'clock? Are you going to get it?" She pushed her hair back as Emma blinked from her pillow.

With a loud sigh, Emma flung the bedclothes aside and covered a sleepy Marms in the process. She padded to her luggage and dug for clothes. Tina hurried back to her own room to get presentable. Emma jerked on jeans she'd worn the day before and scrambled into a worn T-shirt. She ignored the need for shoes and ran out the door.

Hurrying down the stairs, Emma's bare feet slapped against the marble. "Coming!" she yelled at the doorbell's third chime.

Narrow windows sat alongside the front entry, and as Emma gained momentum flying down the steps, she lost control and hit the floor running. Her speed carried her across the foyer, where she was plastered against the window. The impact was noticeable outside as the older man and woman both turned to look, their faces surprised, then concerned, as Emma struggled upright. She gave them a brief smile, then disappeared from the window to open the door.

"Hi," Emma said to the couple. "Sorry you had to wait; it took me a while to get to the door."

The woman spoke first. "Oh, that's quite all right, dear. We've probably called a bit early for you. I hope we didn't get you out of bed." She was smiling broadly at Emma, apparently delighted to meet her and not really sorry for any inconvenience. She had a broad, happy face and laugh crinkles around her sparkling eyes. A floral print dress was lightly tied at her ample waist. Around her head, she wore a simple kerchief, a matching shade of yellow to her dress.

A man stood behind and to the right of the woman, slightly taller, with a rangy build and dark coloring of someone who spent his hours working outdoors. He smiled, too, but didn't have the same enthusiasm in his eyes as his wife. His well-worn jeans and denim shirt sleeves were rolled up to his elbows. He clutched a sweat-stained bushwhacker's hat in his hand. His other hand, he stretched toward Emma.

"I'm James O'Malley, and this here's my wife, Helen. We wanted to come over and make you feel welcome."

Emma shook his hand. Her gaze roamed to the

basket Mrs. O'Malley was holding in front of her. "Emma Stone. Glad to meet you. Would you like to come in?"

Mrs. O'Malley smiled even broader if that were possible. As she entered the house, her husband behind her, she told Emma, "I just knew you'd be hungry this mornin', so I made you some blueberry muffins. I also have some banana bread if you don't like muffins."

The older woman bustled off toward the kitchen, and the scent of her baked goods wafted up and out of the basket directly to Emma. She practically floated behind the couple.

Mrs. O'Malley set the baked goods on the table, and Emma tentatively raised a corner of the bright blue squared napkin covering the basket. Indeed, there was an abundance of huge blueberry muffins and a large loaf of banana bread. Emma took a deep breath, eyes closed in bliss, as she savored the scent. She opened them to find Mrs. O'Malley had filled a coffee filter with grounds, ready to brew.

Mr. O'Malley watched Emma, smiling slightly. "My wife does bake some awfully good homemade muffins and bread." He pulled out a chair for Emma and indicated she should sit. "Not that I want to tell you what to do in your own home, but I'd sit down and have a few of those while they're warm."

"Oh, thank you very much," Emma was about to dive in when she remembered her manners. "Oh, please, have a seat. Mrs. O'Malley, you don't have to do that. Mr. O'Malley, please sit and make yourself at home."

She hurried to the older woman and tried to take the coffee pot away from her as she filled it with water, only to have her shake her hand and shush her away. "I can finish making coffee. Right now, I probably know this place better than you do, and I want to do this." She pushed the start button. "You sit down and enjoy." She reached into the cupboard, withdrew three plates and cups, and placed them in the center of the table.

Tina arrived, making ecstatic noises about the aroma coming from the kitchen. Mrs. O'Malley removed another plate and cup for Tina while Emma pushed the basket of goodies toward her.

After the coffee brewed, the housekeeper poured a cup for each of them, then sat down to enjoy the sweet fare and get to know Emma Stone.

****

After enjoying a plentiful supply of muffins, Tina made an excuse to return to her room. Mr. and Mrs. O'Malley gently approached Emma about their positions at the estate. It was clear they both wanted to keep working there, as housekeeper and cook and groundskeeper and overall handyman.

Emma didn't know what to tell them. "I've never been in the position of employer. I have always been the employee. And this is just my second day. I've only spent one night in this house. I have a lot to think about.

"I'm not making any promises, but I need time myself to figure out what I'm doing. Let's take it a month at a time. And if I think we'll be coming to a parting of the ways, I'll let you know at least a month in advance." Mr. O'Malley seemed to accept these terms, but Mrs. O'Malley's face fell at the thought she might lose her job. Emma added, to cheer her, "Mr. Johnson thinks I should keep you both on." Mrs. O'Malley smiled slightly.

"I want to know what you both do around here."

125

Emma grabbed a pen and paper from a drawer. "Okay, Mr. O'Malley. What do you do here? Are your hours set? Are you flexible?"

****

Emma spent the day with the O'Malleys. Mrs. O'Malley showed her more extensively throughout the house, explained why some things were kept here, others there, and what was personal to Mr. Kerwood, and discussed things for the charity to pick up. After they finished with the house, the housekeeper offered to go to the grocery store for supplies and make them a simple meatloaf dinner. Tina asked to go along, and the two of them left together, chattering as if they'd known each other for a lifetime. Tina didn't hold back when it came to chatting up a new acquaintance, and apparently, Mrs. O'Malley didn't either.

After they left, Mr. O'Malley showed Emma the estate grounds and explained his duties more thoroughly. They started at the front, with the long circular driveway made of crushed white pea gravel. "Mr. Kerwood considered changing this to asphalt many times," he explained. "But he never did. He'd always say he just liked the way this little white rock looked."

As they walked around the main residence, Emma saw the cottages in the back of the property and asked if those were where the O'Malleys and the nurse, Nancy Karroll, lived.

"Yeah." Mr. O'Malley pointed to the house whose lights had come on the evening before. "The missus and I have that place, and Ms. Karroll lives over there." He indicated the other house on the left. "She's still there, but I think she's planning to move. She doesn't talk much to us." He waved toward the residence in the center, the one that was vacant. "Would you like to see inside it, see what they look like? They're all built the same."

"Sure." He took off down the pathway, and Emma hurried to catch up with him. "What's the nurse doing now?"

"Don't know. Haven't seen her since Mr. Kerwood died. We hear she's thinking of building out on that land Mr. Kerwood left her but haven't heard for sure one way or another."

"Is she married?" A husband hadn't been mentioned at any time in relation to the nurse.

"Nope. She's got a brother that comes around now and then, but that's all the family we know of. She keeps pretty quiet."

He opened the back door to the home he and his wife shared and snagged a set of keys off the key rack, then headed toward the empty house. "I'd gladly show you our place, but the missus would probably put me in the doghouse. I think it's clean enough, but she never thinks so."

He wandered around to the front of the house, and Emma followed in his wake. She wondered why they didn't just go in the back since it was handier. It was as if he read her mind.

"It's bad luck to go in a house for the first time through the back door, ya know." He rattled the key in the doorknob, looking back at her while he did so. "That's why we walked all the way around here."

He took her on a short tour through the partially furnished little house. Afterward, he took her on a more extended tour of the estate via a motorized cart that was housed in a barn situated away from the houses. There was a path carved out in the woods, and the little vehicle could take them to most of the land. Mr. Kerwood had kept cattle at one time when he was younger, so about fifty acres of the property was devoted to a pasture area with a quiet, tree-shaded pond in its center. They had also kept horses. They had been sold when the Kerwoods weren't physically capable of riding anymore.

When Emma returned to the house, Mrs. O'Malley and Tina were busy putting up groceries. Emma sat in the kitchen and chatted with them while they put things away in an organized manner.

"Oh!" Emma suddenly remembered her impromptu dinner with Detective Wells on Saturday. "Mrs. O'Malley, I'm sorry, but I already have a favor to ask you to do for me." She grinned sheepishly as Mrs. O'Malley turned to her. She explained about inviting Detective Wells for dinner on a sudden impulse and hoped that Mrs. O'Malley could whip up an impressive meal.

"Of course, dear! I'd be delighted to cook something special for you. What would you like?" Mrs. O'Malley was beaming with anticipation.

Coming from a family of down-to-earth food and her own cooking skills being minimal, Emma didn't have a clue. She hadn't thought to ask the detective what he liked. "I really don't know. I didn't ask if he had a preference."

"Then might I suggest a simple pot roast? When you don't know what your dinner guests like, that's hard to beat. Or if you want to impress him a bit more, how about prime rib?" Since Mr. Kerwood had rarely entertained the last several years of his life, Mrs. O'Malley's opportunities to cook a full meal, complete with appetizers and dessert, had become slim. She was ecstatic at the thought of cooking for the couple.

"And will you be staying, Miss Tina? Or do you have a young man of your own to join in for dinner?"

Tina was headed to the pantry with an armload of paper towels. She looked at Emma. She didn't want to be the third wheel. "Uh, no. I won't be here Saturday." Speaking slowly but thinking rapidly, Tina made eye contact with Emma. "In fact, I plan to visit my parents. I'll be back Sunday sometime."

"Well, then, Miss Emma," Mrs. O'Malley happily chirped, "as soon as we have these things put away, we'll put together a full menu for your Saturday night dinner."

Chapter Fourteen

The next couple of days slipped by in a pleasant blur. Emma and Tina shopped at the mall in Joplin, explored the Grove area, and took walks in the woods around the estate. Having been such good friends for years, they were comfortable with each other. And both expected Tina wouldn't be staying indefinitely with Emma. As of yet, Tina had not made any other plans. She considered applying for a teaching position in the local school system, a plan Emma encouraged.

On Wednesday morning, Emma made a phone call to a local charity service, and they arranged for a truck to come early Thursday afternoon and pick up a variety of Mr. Kerwood's personal items and furniture. The men spent the afternoon loading up furniture from the den/bedroom, including the bedroom suite and even the red plaid recliner that listed to the side.

After loading all they could get in their truck that day, they determined they would come back the next morning to finish. Emma hadn't thought there would be that much stuff, but when it was removed from the den and upstairs, it turned out to be quite a bit of furniture, bedding, and clothes. They emptied the master closets, so Emma could hang her own clothing.

Friday morning dawned beautiful, another cool autumn day. The donation truck arrived, and Emma left Tina with the loaders to pick up the items they'd set aside the night before and to show the guys upstairs.

The third floor hadn't been investigated, and Emma decided it was time. Hurrying through the second-floor center hallway to the back staircase, Emma opened the door at the foot of the stairs. A light switch at the bottom illuminated the stairway.

She cautiously climbed the stairs. Closed off from the rest of the house, the third floor was quiet. The air was stale since the furnace and air conditioner vents were currently shut.

The top of the stairs opened into a hallway similar to the second floor. There were two tables in the hallway, unadorned by flowers as on the floor below.

Emma peeked in each room quickly, then hurried down. There were four large bedrooms, and all were furnished. She saw enough to know it needed a more thorough look and a return visit from the charity truck.

After the truck had been loaded and rumbled down the drive, Tina went to pack for her trip to her parents. She'd called them, and they were looking forward to her overnight stay.

Emma wandered into the house behind Tina. Their paths split when Tina went upstairs, and Emma continued through the dining room to stand and look out the French doors. She opened them and walked onto the patio.

Marms, who now had run of the house and occasionally went outside, meowed loudly and scampered out with her. Emma sat down in a two-seater patio glider, and before she could put it into movement, Marms leaped alongside her. She reached over and pulled him onto her lap, rubbing her cheek against his big yellow head.

"What d'ya think, Marms?" She scratched behind his ear, and he purred. "We've got a pretty good life here, don't we?" From her vantage point, she could look over the rolling hills and see the lake in the distance. The water was a deep blue, a few whitecaps shown as the wind ruffled the waves. The autumn-tinged air was cool, and the western breeze stirred the leaves on the trees around the house.

She took a deep breath, then let it out slowly. The air was intoxicating. It felt like fall, it smelled like fall, and fall was her favorite time of the year. After the hot, humid summers in Oklahoma, nothing felt as refreshing to Emma as a cool, crisp autumn day.

They sat together, Emma and Marms, content to watch birds and feel the cool breeze. Emma's foot gently pushed against the stone patio, and the glider moved in a smooth back-and-forth motion. *Yes, life is good.*

****

Saturday morning, Tina put her overnight bag and a small cooler of colas in her little car, gave Emma a brief hug, and waved goodbye to Mrs. O'Malley as she rolled down the driveway.

Emma thought Tina seemed happy to go off for a couple of days and visit her parents. She hadn't seen them in a few months and was looking forward to spending some time with them.

"You don't need to make breakfast this morning, Mrs. O'Malley," Emma told her as they re-entered the house. "With your good cooking, I've been eating way too much lately. I can't keep it up. My jeans are getting tighter already." She wedged her finger into her waistband to make her point.

"Nonsense," the housekeeper waved her hand in

dismissal. "You're such a pretty, skinny young lady. You have room to put some meat on your bones."

Emma followed her into the kitchen and plucked a can of soda from the refrigerator. "I appreciate the compliment, but the fact remains. I'll just have some toast and jelly this morning. That way, if there's anything you need to do before Mike gets here, you don't have to bother with me." She popped her can and took a sip. "I think he'll be here early this afternoon."

For the life of her, she couldn't see where anything needed to be done, but she had learned where Mrs. O'Malley was concerned, the place couldn't be clean enough. Things were always in their place. It would be a most irritating situation, except for the woman's cheerful disposition. Undaunted by a casual throw of the sweater over a piece of furniture, the minute your back was turned, the housekeeper would have that sweater swooped up and hung in a closet.

Emma finished her toast and rinsed off her plate when the doorbell rang. *Who could that be?*

Hurrying to the front door, Emma peeked out the side window. An attractive blonde woman in her mid-thirties waited, casually dressed in the sharp manner of those who have money and spend it on their appearance. Her hair was short and neatly coiffed, and Emma guessed the color was a professional job, no do-it-yourself at-home box job.

Emma opened the door and greeted her guest with a cheerful "Good morning."

The woman smiled, a smile that didn't quite reach her eyes. She held out her hand to Emma, "I'm Nancy Karroll. I was Mr. Kerwood's nurse. I wanted to come by and meet the new owner."

"Oh!" Emma's eyebrows shot up. While curious to meet Ms. Karroll, she didn't expect her to show up on the doorstep unannounced. "Please come in."

As Emma led the way to the living room, she asked the woman if she would like something to drink.

"If Mrs. O'Malley has made some coffee, that would be nice," Ms. Karroll sat on one of the sofas and looked around the room. "I see you've made a few changes already."

"Just donated some furniture and things. I'll get the coffee, be right back." Emma hurried out and had set the coffee pot and cups on a tray when Mrs. O'Malley entered the room. At her inquiring look, Emma explained that Ms. Karroll dropped by for a visit.

"Oh, she has, has she? Well, you keep an eye on her, Miss Emma, and don't go telling her anything you don't want her to know. She hasn't been around since Mr. Kerwood died." She sniffed in irritation. "And Mr. Kerwood treated her well for no longer than she had been with him."

"Okay, thanks." Emma balanced the tray, carried it into the living room, and placed it on the long coffee table between the two sofas.

Marms had wandered in while Emma was getting the drinks, and if a cat could frown, Marms was frowning. He stared at Ms. Karroll, his eyes in slits, as if willing her to leave. Marms was usually hot or cold. He either liked you or disliked you. Emma had to admit the big grumpy cat disliked most people, but in Ms. Karroll's case, it looked like an active hatred building up.

Ms. Karroll still sat where Emma left her and smiled as Emma put the tray down. She completely ignored Marms, which Emma imagined irritated the cat even more.

"Do you like it here, Miss Stone?" Ms. Karroll asked as her drink was poured. Emma pushed the cup toward her. Ms. Karroll reached for the cream and sugar and put a generous amount in her cup.

"What's not to like?" Emma queried back. "The place is beautiful. It's quiet, the town is nice…"

"But it's not a city like Tulsa. Your friends aren't here."

Emma sipped and looked at her guest, suddenly defensive. "Tulsa's not that far. My friends can find me easily enough. Besides…" She sat her cup down and looked at the nurse. "I've been here less than a week. I'm sure I'll adjust. What are your plans?" Emma hoped she wasn't too blunt, but she wanted to know. If Nancy Karroll didn't want to tell her, that was okay. In the meantime, the nurse was living in a house on Emma's property. Emma thought she had some right to nosiness.

"Mr. Kerwood left me some property on the edge of town and some money, enough to build a house. I may do that." She looked at Emma. "I'm sure you know that Mr. Kerwood's will stipulated that I could live here up to six months while I decide what to do. I'll need to stay here while the new house is being built." She gave Emma a slight smile over the edge of her coffee cup. "I hope that's not a problem."

"No, of course not."

Silence grew between them as they sipped their coffee.

"What was Mr. Kerwood like?" Emma asked. The O'Malleys painted him as a quiet man, generous and soft-hearted. She wondered if his nurse saw him in the same light.

"I hate to speak ill of the dead, but I didn't particularly think he was a nice man." She sat her cup down and looked Emma straight in the eye. "That's probably not what the O'Malleys are telling you, is it?"

"Uh, no. They seem to think he was pretty nice." Emma cradled her coffee cup in her hands as she studied the nurse. The woman's appearance indicated she was doing well financially. "How long had you worked for him?"

"Five years. But that was long enough." She sat her drink down and abruptly stood up. "I left some personal items here, in the downstairs bathroom. If you wouldn't mind, I'd like to get them."

Surprised and grateful at her guest's announcement that she intended to gather her items and presumably leave, Emma rose to her feet as well. They were not finding much in common to discuss. "Of course. Well, you know where the bathroom is, and I don't think anything has been removed. We've already cleaned out Mr. Kerwood's bedroom downstairs. I hope you didn't have anything there." She didn't remember anything of a feminine nature in that room.

"No, I'll just be a minute and be out of your way." The nurse briskly walked out of the room and headed to the solitary downstairs bathroom.

Emma stood alone, slightly uncomfortable. *Should I follow her? Make sure she doesn't steal something? Is there anything to steal?* She couldn't remember any particular items of importance in the bathroom. Emma didn't want to hover, yet she didn't feel comfortable giving Ms. Karroll free rein either. She walked to the foot of the staircase and waited. When the nurse emerged from the bathroom to leave, Emma would be there to politely escort her out. That seemed a reasonable solution.

She waited patiently for what seemed like a very long time when, in essence, it was only a couple of minutes. Marms also strolled into the entry to wait with her. His tail swished back and forth in a slow rhythm. Emma glanced at her watch for a second time, resisting the urge to tap her foot. Finally, she ambled toward the bathroom.

Ms. Karroll was moving things about; sounds of rattling and clinking floated out of the room.

"Find what you need?" Emma couldn't resist asking and felt a slight satisfaction at the nervous jump from the nurse.

"Yes, I believe this is all." Ms. Karroll turned around, some toiletry items in her hands and her purse rounder than before. "Do you mind if I come back if I've forgotten anything?"

"Of course not." Emma was surprised she even asked. "It's your stuff. You should have it."

"Thank you. I'll just be going now." The nurse walked to leave, Emma close behind. Before she left, the woman turned to Emma. "It was nice to meet you," she said with what appeared to be true sincerity. "And I really do hope you will be happy here."

"Thank you," was all Emma could think to say as she felt puzzled over the woman's appearance and abrupt departure. She had the uneasy feeling that she had been studied, appraised, and found wanting.

A cheery red convertible waited in the driveway. Ms. Karroll opened the passenger side first to deposit her toiletry items, then went around to the driver's door. She gave Emma a little smile and goodbye wave, then slid in the car and drove around to the separate drive that led to the cottages.

Emma strolled back inside, picked up the tray of lukewarm coffee, and returned it to the kitchen. Mrs. O'Malley was back in the utility room, doing some last-minute laundry for one of the extra bedrooms upstairs. Emma had suggested they might have an extra room ready should Mike decide to stay overnight. It also set a good example for her to the older woman, as she was certain the housekeeper would frown on the thought of Mike staying without a bed of his own to sleep in. And in fact, Emma did not anticipate him spending the night, but well, you never know.

Mrs. O'Malley bustled into the kitchen as Emma rinsed the cups. As the old washer churned in the background, Marms trotted into the utility room. The housekeeper grudgingly accepted the big cat, as Emma made it clear Marms was staying and had run of the house. However, Marms learned it was in his best interest to steer clear of the older woman, at least until her heart warmed toward him. Marms seemed to like Mrs. O'Malley just fine, but his cat's sixth sense told him to hold back a little and not push it.

Mr. O'Malley was a different matter. From the beginning, they had gotten along famously. The older man seldom sat down while in the house, but if he did, Marms was there to weave around his feet, seeming to realize that he wouldn't be welcome as a lap cat. After the first few days, Emma let him out the back door, and Marms had soon become comfortable around the estate, occasionally following Mr. O'Malley as he went about his landscaping chores.

Emma looked up from her dishwashing. "Ms.

Karroll is gone. She just had some personal things to get, she said."

"Humph" was all she heard Mrs. O'Malley respond. She opened the refrigerator to get the roast for the evening meal. Emma leaned back against the counter and studied her. The older woman bustled about, set the roast down, then wiped her hands on a towel tied to her apron strings.

"It's obvious you don't like her," Emma said. "Why?" Her very short conversation with the nurse had left her confused. She sensed that Nancy Karroll was ready to leave her position with Mr. Kerwood, and his timely death fit into her plans well. There was something about her she didn't quite like, but she couldn't put her finger on it. Perhaps Mrs. O'Malley, in her simple country sense of priorities, could explain.

The housekeeper/cook stopped in front of the roast and turned to Emma, her hands on each of her ample hips. A simple full-length apron in a pattern of bright red apples, blushing peaches, and yellow-green pears was wrapped around her. It fit right with her nature, and Emma could picture her at her sewing machine, stitching it together. "If you know what I mean when I say she would give herself airs, then that's what I mean."

Emma ran this through her mind and wrinkled her forehead. "She acted like she was better than you?"

Mrs. O'Malley had grabbed the kitchen shears and proceeded to slice open the roast package. "That's right, dear. And she never acted or indicated she *wanted* to fit in. No sittin' around the kitchen table for that one."

"I see." The nurse and housekeeper would never have gotten along. Since they would soon be parting ways, she couldn't see where it was of any consequence at this point.

"Mike might show up a little early. I think I'll go outside for a bit, maybe watch for him."

Marms had taken a few bites out of his food bowl and wandered back into the room over to Emma. She scooped him up and headed out of the dining room. As she passed one of the tables in the entry, she noticed her cell phone lying there and grabbed it, too. Just in case Mike got lost and had to call her. With Marms and her cell phone in hand, she fumbled with the front doors, opening them to step out in the sunny afternoon.

There was a white-painted wrought iron loveseat with cushions to the side of the entry door, and Emma settled down with Marms to wait and soak up the sunshine. It was a beautiful day, and she turned her face upward, seeking the sun's warmth. Autumn crispness was in the air. A slight breeze ruffled her hair, blowing a tiny tendril across her face.

Marms, beside her, curled around for a perfect catnap in the sun. She reached over and absent-mindedly rubbed his head. He stretched a front paw out while she rubbed him, then curled back up again.

Her cell phone went off, the theme song from a favorite sitcom. Emma answered, knowing it was Tina. She called Emma to advise she'd arrived at her parents' safe and sound.

"Has Mike arrived yet?" Tina asked.

"No, and I wish he would get here. I know it's early. He's not supposed to be here this soon. But I am so *bored*." She sighed heavily. "There's no last-minute shopping to do, the house is spotless, Mrs. O'Malley is cooking dinner, and I even checked cable TV, and there's nothing I want to watch." She hitched her foot up on the seat and leaned her arm against her knee as she talked to her friend. "I'm hoping when he gets here, he can tell me something about the case. I don't know if he's allowed to talk about it to me, but I'm going to ask him anyway. I'd like to think they've found Malone by now, although nothing has been on the news about it. I'm still scared to think that he may be out there, and he could find out where I am and come after me."

"Did he ever suggest you might talk to Mr. Sun's widow?" Tina asked. "Maybe she would feel a little comfort, talking to the last person to see her husband alive."

"Mrs. Sun? No, he never suggested it. I think he wants me to stay as low profile as possible. He was irritated that the media let out that there was a witness. He called this morning for directions and asked again if I had seen anyone that I would call suspicious. I told him, no, it was quiet here."

Emma looked down the driveway, thinking she saw movement. Maybe that was Mike coming early, after all.

A dark blue sedan continued up the driveway, parking at the bottom of the steps to the house. Emma waved when she saw Mike behind the wheel.

"Tina, Mike's here. I'll talk to you later," and hung up.

She stood, and her movement woke Marms, who yawned and looked to see what had disturbed his nap. Seeing it was Mike, he stretched and sat, ready to be petted.

Chapter Fifteen

Nancy Karroll put away her things from Emma's and realized she had forgotten to look in the bottom of the vanity to see if she had left anything there. Her curling iron was still unaccounted for.

This time, she would walk over to the main house and get the curler, not bothering to drive. It was a short distance, and it would feel good to stretch her legs.

She slipped on walking shoes to make the journey more comfortable. As she rounded the front of the house, she could see Emma sitting on the iron loveseat, the big yellow cat curled beside her. Emma's back was to her. The position of her head indicated she was on the phone.

Emma's voice drifted to her, confirming her impression. She heard the words "Mrs. Sun." Her curiosity piqued, she stopped and listened.

Emma was talking about the robbery and Mr. Sun being killed. There could be no doubt about it. As what Emma was saying sank in, Nancy slowly backed away, easing around the side of the house before she could be seen. She stopped for a moment once she was certain she was out of Emma's sight and looked around to see if anyone else had noticed her. All was quiet.

The nurse returned to her house, almost tripping in her haste. As she unlocked her back door, she checked out the window again. No one was in sight.

She grabbed her purse, dug out her cell phone, and

punched a speed dial number. She stood, shifting from foot to foot, finally pacing as she anxiously waited for her call to be answered. When voice mail picked up, she said simply. "That witness you were looking for? I know who and where. Call me."

****

Emma greeted Mike with a big smile and opened her arms wide. "Welcome to my humble abode."

Mike shut the driver's door and studied the grand house. Emma stood there, arms out and a huge smile on her face. He didn't know which was more impressive, the gorgeous young woman or the residence behind her. The smile still in place, she trotted down the steps to him.

His gaze was glued to her face. He had forgotten how pretty she was. Forcing himself to look away and back at the house, he noted. "This really is beautiful. Is it big enough for you?" he joked.

"Yeah. Tina and I and the O'Malleys bump into each other occasionally, though. I've been thinking of adding a wing. What do you think?"

"Well, there's that to be considered. Don't want to be too crowded." He started up the steps. "Seriously, how have you been?"

He was as nice to look at as she remembered, although his dark blue eyes were worried. Emma wanted to reach out and touch him, reassure him she was fine. It had been a week since they met at the crime scene, and their relationship, if you could call it that, was strictly professional. Although she hoped it didn't stay that way.

Mike reached out to her first as he went up the steps, sliding his arm around her in a casual touch. He gave her shoulder a brief squeeze as they ascended to the porch, then looked down at her. "You look good," he said simply.

"I'm doing great," Emma replied. She pulled an errant lock of hair out of her face and tucked it away. As he turned and looked at her, she continued, "It's good to be here. It's quiet. Nothing has happened. No strangers lurking in the attic or the bushes. Just me, Tina, and the O'Malleys." She thought a bit. "Oh, and Mr. Kerwood's ex-nurse and the donation guys." She pursed her lips, thinking. "I think that's it. Very quiet life here."

They walked together to the iron loveseat, where Marms patiently waited. Mike reached out and gave the cat a rub on the head.

"In fact," Emma continued as they sat down, "I tend to forget that I have to be on the watch for Malone. I catch the news at night to see if there is anything new about Mr. Sun's murder, hoping you've caught him. The O'Malleys are great. I love both of them already." She paused. "It's kinda like living with your parents again, but not quite. They're only here during the day, and Mr. O'Malley spends a lot of his time outside, so I don't see him much." Her eyes turned serious and hopeful. "*Have* you had any luck catching Malone?"

"We've had call-ins, tips, questionable sightings, whatever you want to call them, but nothing that has led us to him yet." His eyes turned serious too. "It's not easy, and he's very good. He's a career criminal, a jewel thief who's stolen for years and never been caught. And he would have gotten away with it this time if you hadn't happened to see him."

"And I kick myself every time I think about how I hesitated to come forward about him. I was scared he was coming after me. But if I had, it might have been easier. Maybe he hadn't even left town yet. Now we don't know where he is."

"Well, if our tips are anything to go on, and I use the term *tips* lightly, we believe he is still in the Tulsa area, maybe Oklahoma City."

"I wonder why he hasn't left."

Mike idly reached over and scratched Marms on the head. The big cat closed his eyes in bliss. "Umm," was all he mumbled while Emma looked at him, her eyes narrowing. He didn't want to have to spell it out for her. She was smart. She'd get it.

"It's me, isn't it?" She could tell by his uncomfortable look she was right. "He knows I'm out here somewhere, can identify him, and is hanging around trying to find me." She watched him closely, hoping she was wrong.

He nodded, and her heart sank. "You're right," he said. "Ever since it leaked on the news that there was a witness, it has been our belief that he won't leave the area until he knows you're not around to testify against him."

As his words sank in, Emma blinked. She would *not* show weakness. She looked at Mike, her face serious. "What am I supposed to do? Just stay hidden? For how long?"

He didn't answer her immediately. When he did, it wasn't what she hoped to hear. "I don't know. If he remains at large, you are a target. I just hope he never finds out who you are and where you live." He looked hopeful. "But, on a bright note, the sheriff and police in Grove and Delaware County have been very helpful and willing to do all they can to protect you. They just have limited manpower. There'd be a deputy or officer on your doorstep every night if they could."

Emma nodded, looking down at the ground. "I

know," she said. "I met the police chief and a couple of deputies. They were nice and offered help if I needed it."

A brief silence grew, both uncomfortable with the strained situation. Emma sighed and turned to Mike, a forced smile on her face. "Well. Nothing can be done right here and now about a killer possibly lurking around waiting for me, so why don't I take you on a tour of the estate? This really is an incredible place."

"Great. Part of what I'm here for—to know where you are at all times." He grinned, and she relaxed and smiled back at him.

"And what is the other part of why you're here?" she asked as she stood, trying to decide where to start his tour. Her gaze remained on him, and he looked a little uncomfortable.

"Strictly personal." He looked her straight in the eyes and unblushingly told her, "I want to get to know you better."

"Oh." A warmth crept up her face. "That's nice," Emma blurted. Realizing she needed to contribute more, she added, "I'd like to know you better too, and it's lucky we have all weekend, uh, or whatever." Stammering, she decided to change the subject back to her tour. "What would you like to see first, inside or out?" Her face glowed, and she was determined to ignore it. When she looked at him, and he was trying to keep from laughing at her discomfort, she decided to just give in to it. "Is it hot out here?"

He laughed out loud, a healthy sound that made her smile bigger.

"Seriously, you are welcome to stay if you like. There's plenty of room and chaperones waiting in the wings."

"Chaperones?" he puzzled. "Who? Tina?"

"No. The O'Malleys. Remember them? Like parents? Tina isn't here now; she went off to spend the weekend with her folks."

He turned and looked out over the circle driveway and the front of the house. It was a gorgeous autumn day. He stated maybe they should start the tour with the outside since the weather was so nice.

Emma nodded, reached over, and scratched Marms on the head. "See you later, fella." She led the way around the side of the house. Marms jumped down to sidle along with them.

They took a leisurely tour around the lawn. Emma pointed out her favorite patio at the side of the house overlooking the estate and, far away, the lake. "It's more private," she explained. "It comes off the dining room and has this gorgeous view. The back patio is nice too, but it faces the three houses, and I feel like I can be seen while I'm there. The rear of the other houses face the patio of the main house."

"What do you mean, main house, and what other houses?" Mike hadn't received a layout of the house and grounds and didn't realize there were companion houses to the estate.

Emma explained. "The O'Malley's and the nurse occupied two of the three houses behind the estate. I understand the houses were designed as an in-law house, guests, whoever needed them. And before Mr. Kerwood died, that meant a nurse and housekeeper and groundskeeper."

She led the way and pointed out how the manicured grounds showed Mr. O'Malley's meticulous care. Except for the occasional bird song, the grounds were quiet.

Mike couldn't see how one could feel watched here. Looking around, the woods were dense and could hide someone, but far enough away to be non-threatening. However, when they approached the rear of Emma's place, it was evident.

The three houses were lined up like sentinels across the back of the property. They were far enough away to maintain privacy, yet someone looking out a window of one of the guest houses could easily see anyone on the back patio of the main house.

"I see what you mean," he said. "I feel exposed."

"Yeah." Emma agreed. "I don't feel comfortable in this area, so I don't come out here often. But I'm sure I'll feel better with time." They circled around the side of the house and back to the front. Emma led him up to the front door and started to open it.

Mike reached out and held out a hand to stop her. "There wasn't that much left to see. Why didn't we just go in the back door when we were there?"

Emma grinned. "The entry is much more impressive than the laundry room."

"Ahhh." He leaned his head back. "I see." He waved at the door handle. "Well then, let's go in. Through the front door."

Emma grabbed both door handles and pushed inward in a grand gesture. "Welcome."

Mike's reaction was much like Emma's when she first saw the inside of the house. He did not appear awestruck, but he was impressed. "Very nice," he mumbled, "very, very nice."

Marms scuttled in front of them. Emma led the way into the living room, then opened the double doors to the dining room. The succulent aroma of roast beef wafted over the couple.

"What is that wonderful smell?" Mike inhaled deeply and leaned toward the scent. Marms trotted through ahead. He would take his chances with Mrs. O'Malley for a taste of beef.

Mike looked suspiciously at Emma. "Are you cooking something? I thought you didn't cook."

"I don't. Mrs. O'Malley is cooking pot roast for our dinner. An early one, I hope," she added as her mouth watered. "Come on, I'll introduce you. You'll like her." She led the way through the dining room to the warm kitchen.

"Mrs. O'Malley? I'd like you to meet Mike Wells."

The older woman turned from the stove to greet him and dried her hands on a dishtowel.

"Mike is a detective with the Tulsa police department," Emma added as the two shook hands. Mrs. O'Malley grinned, and her eyes crinkled in delight.

Mike smiled and nodded. "Whatever you're cooking smells delicious. Emma says it might be our dinner."

"Indeed, it is, and I hope you like pot roast." She waved at the stove where a couple of other things heated. "I could do fancy, but not knowing your preference, decided to keep it simple, so pot roast it is." She glanced at the clock built into the stovetop. "It should be ready in another hour or so. Hope you're hungry." She beamed.

"I didn't know how hungry I was until I smelled that. I can hardly wait."

He turned to Emma, who waited patiently. "You ready to continue the tour? You might have to listen to my stomach growling." He hadn't eaten all day, and the caffeine from the coffee he drank earlier was wearing thin.

"Follow me." Emma led him out of the dining room and into the refurbished den and library.

As she chatted away, something gnawed at Mike, and it had nothing to do with hunger. He missed something, and he couldn't quite put his finger on what. While he hadn't been a detective for too many years, he had learned to listen to his instincts, his gut. Now, that same gut was waving, shouting, and whistling to get his attention.

Emma stopped her chatter. "What's wrong?" Mike seemed distracted, and he had a preoccupied frown on his face. "Did I say something wrong?"

"No, you're fine. It's just…there's something, I can't explain it, but I feel like there's something right in front of me, and I don't get it. And it's important." His face cleared, and he turned to Emma. "Have the O'Malleys been with Mr. Kerwood long?"

"Yes. Many years. Why?"

"I need to talk to your cook again."

Chapter Sixteen

Mike turned, walked out of the library, and headed back to the kitchen. Emma hurried to keep up.

"What about her?" Emma grabbed hold of his arm, stopping him. "You can't tell me she's involved in the killing or robbery. The O'Malleys are the sweetest people on Earth."

"I have to ask her something." He shook her loose and hurried out of the room. Emma scurried behind.

"Mrs. O'Malley!" Mike barked her name as he entered the kitchen, startling the older woman as she was arranging potatoes in a baking pan. Her eyes grew big in response to the severe look he shot her.

"What?" She gasped.

"Do you have relatives in Tulsa?"

Puzzled, she answered immediately. "No." She added, "Most of our family is east, and Kathleen, our daughter, lives in Wisconsin. Why?"

He ignored her question. "Do you ever go to Tulsa?"

"Well, of course. It's only a couple of hours away. I like to do my Christmas shopping there. Why?"

He persisted. "Have you ever been to a jeweler in downtown Tulsa, Sun Jewelry?"

Emma was intrigued. She looked at him and frowned. "Mike, they couldn't."

"No. I thought it might be something else."

Mrs. O'Malley was staring at him, puzzled.

151

He turned and whispered to Emma, "There was a receipt for repair found with Mr. Sun, with the name Omal on it."

"Oh." Emma held up a finger to Mike. "Mrs. O'Malley," she said, and turned to the housekeeper. "Didn't you mention that you or Mr. O'Malley ran errands for Mr. Kerwood?"

The cook dropped the final potatoes in the pan and wiped her hands on the dish towel again. "Well, yes. All the time. My husband usually did."

"Do you think he would have gone within…" At this she turned and looked at Mike as she didn't know the time frame they were working within.

"…the last few months," he filled in for her.

Mrs. O'Malley nodded, "I believe he did. He didn't tell me what the trip was for, although he usually does. He said Mr. Kerwood was kinda private about it. It didn't concern me, so I didn't ask any questions." She shrugged her shoulders as if that were the end of that.

Mike was enthused. Possibly this wasn't a dead-end after all. Maybe it wasn't a coincidence that the name Omal had come up at the crime scene and right under his nose as he visited Emma. "Mrs. O'Malley," he asked, "where is your husband now?"

"Probably at the house since he isn't here. I'll call and see," she said as she reached for the phone. When he answered, she nodded at Mike and Emma. "He's home."

Mike turned to Emma. "Take me there."

"Sure." She waved at Mrs. O'Malley, who explained to her husband that Emma and Mike were coming to see him right away.

As they rushed out of the kitchen, she yelled, "He said he'd meet you at the back door."

"Thanks!" Emma called back. Mike held her hand and pulled her along, in a hurry but not quite running. On the patio, he paused. "Which one is theirs?"

Emma pointed toward the middle house as Mr. O'Malley opened the back door and looked their way. He raised his hand in a friendly wave, and the two started toward him.

"I still don't get it," Emma panted as they hurried forward. "There was a receipt in Mr. Sun's stuff that had Omal on it. So what?"

Mike slowed his pace. "Mr. Sun had some things he was working on. He wasn't the best when it came to keeping records of repair items. If Mr. O'Malley left something, and it's not among the things we found, it might be what the killer was after." He looked at her. "See? So, it might be important to know what the item was, if indeed he *had* left something there. This could be a dead end. He could have done something else for Mr. Kerwood, but my gut tells me different. This bears investigating."

They walked to the rear of the O'Malley house, and the older man met them outside on their small patio. Four padded chairs sat around a round glass-top table. Mr. O'Malley set his cup of coffee down as he greeted them.

"Sit down. Can I get you a coffee? Is something wrong?" Mr. O'Malley wasn't sure what to ask first.

Mike looked agitated, and Emma was worried. She shook her head. "No, thank you."

The detective stretched out his hand and introduced himself, and the older man shook it firmly.

"Is something wrong?" Mr. O'Malley repeated. "Helen said this might have to do with an errand I did for Mr. Kerwood." He sipped his coffee in a cup that proclaimed he was Irish and proud of it. He motioned toward the other chairs. "Have a seat. Tell me what this is about."

Mike and Emma sat, and the detective turned his full attention to the older man. "So, you ran errands for Mr. Kerwood? On a regular basis?"

Mr. O'Malley took a sip and swallowed before answering. "Of course. Mr. Kerwood didn't get around so good. I did a lot of things for him."

Mike decided to get right to the point. "Did you take a piece of jewelry to a jeweler in Tulsa, Sun Jewelry?"

"Sure, I did. Except it isn't a piece of jewelry, really." He took another drink. "Mrs. Kerwood had it made into a brooch, and Mr. Kerwood didn't find it until after she died. Apparently, after she had it altered, she never wore it. He'd never seen it, to know what she had done. When he found it, oh, a few months ago, he pitched a fit. Wanted it fixed back the way it was. That's why he had me take it to Mr. Sun to have it repaired. Mr. Sun probably fixed it, but then Mr. Kerwood got really sick and died, and I forgot about it, and didn't think to see if it was done."

He sipped his coffee. "After all, it wasn't mine. Then I saw in the news where Mr. Sun had been killed in a hold-up. That's too bad, he seemed like a nice man."

"Can you describe it to me?"

"Not very pretty at all. I don't know why the missus thought she would wear it. Her previous jeweler had put a pin thingy on the back so she could attach it to her clothes. It was gold and round, had spiky things coming out of it, I guess like the rays of a sun."

He took a final sip of coffee. "Don't know why she didn't tell the mister about it, but she'd get independent like that sometimes. The way he acted when he found it, probably a good thing. He was not happy. Said something about it had to be fixed before he could use it."

"What did he mean by that?" Mike asked.

"I don't know. Mr. Kerwood, the wife, and I, we got along fine if we didn't ask too many questions. He was a good man, but he wasn't one to share private things."

"Do you know how he wanted it repaired?"

"He told me he wanted the pin taken off and the back smooth, just like it had been before."

Mike stood and extended his hand. "Thank you, Mr. O'Malley, you've been very helpful." Emma followed his cue and stood also, ready to leave.

"I hope you find him. The man who killed Mr. Sun, I mean."

"We'll do our best." He hesitated. "Mr. O'Malley?" When the older man answered, Mike continued, "You do lock your doors here, don't you?"

Mr. O'Malley pursed his lips and shook his head. "Not usually, no need to."

"I think there may be a need to, now. Please keep doors locked. Watch for anyone, and I mean *anyone* who's a stranger. That means if a delivery comes from town, watch to see that it's someone you *know.* If it's not, be very careful around them. And spend a lot of time with your wife. I'm going to encourage her not to be outside alone." He paused. "Do you own a gun?"

Mr. O'Malley looked worried now. "Yeah, but just a twenty-two rifle. I used to do a little squirrel and rabbit huntin' now and then."

"You might clean it and keep it close."

"All right," the older man agreed. He spoke slowly,

thoughtfully. "I take it there *is* a problem?"

"Very likely there is." Mike turned to Emma, his eyes serious. "We need to talk."

****

With a hard grip on Emma's hand, Mike practically dragged her across the lawn from the O'Malley's home. Emma struggled to keep up, protesting as they hurried across the sprawling green space. She didn't understand the urgency, and he didn't take time to explain until they were in a safe location.

They reached the back door, and Mike pushed her inside. She wanted him to talk to her while he concentrated on getting them where they were protected.

"In a minute," he told her, which wasn't good enough for Emma.

She raised her voice as she protested. "*What* is going on?"

He shoved the door closed and turned to face an angry Emma. She stood straight and tall, arms crossed, her fierce glare telling him he had some explaining to do. He glanced past her and saw Marms sitting in the kitchen doorway, watching them with interest. He let out a breath. The cat's calm demeanor told him nothing untoward or exciting had happened while they were gone and that no evil men had entered and killed Mrs. O'Malley. Just to be sure, he peeked in the kitchen door to see the lady in question standing before the stove, humming while she stirred a pot. All was well.

He turned to Emma, now tapping her foot. Her brown eyes had narrowed to go along with the frown. She looked beautiful, and he couldn't help but grin, which made her change from frowning to confusion. She marched toward him.

"What is up with you?" She waved her arm toward the back door and the lawn they had crossed so quickly. "You won't tell me anything. Just drag me across the yard. Made me think someone was going to take potshots at us."

His grin went away.

Her anger evaporated. "Oh." She looked down as she thought, then back up at him, only a few inches from her. "Those questions to Mr. O'Malley about strangers, and keeping his doors locked, and his gun. You really *do* think Malone could be after me. He could find me here, in the middle of nowhere?"

"I do now." He reached out and took her hands, wrapping his around them. He stood looking at her, his gaze solemn.

She stared back, deep brown eyes worried. "Why? What haven't you told me?"

"I didn't know it until after we talked to him." He nodded toward Mr. O'Malley's house. "But what he took to have repaired…we *didn't* recover anything like that in the jewelry store. Which means," he added to her confusion, "that Mr. Sun probably was killed to get that brooch."

"So? Why do you think Malone might come here?"

"Because the brooch belonged to Mr. Kerwood."

"So, he got what he wanted. *Why* come here?"

"Because I don't think the brooch is all they want. I think it's just the beginning."

"Oohh…" She stared at him, his hands still gently holding hers. She looked down and closed her eyes, then opened them and looked up at him. "Okay. Now I'm scared." She gave a shaky smile. "So, what do we do? Lock the front door?"

Mike chuckled and leaned forward to give her lips a brief kiss. Despite standing so close, it caught her off guard. Her eyes flashed in surprise, and he smiled. Before she could move away, he leaned in and pressed another kiss on her lips, this one lingering as her hands tightened in his. He broke it off, raised her hands, and brushed his lips across her fingers. His expression was sober as he stood back. Emma smiled as a happy warmth washed over her.

He brushed a strand of hair off her face. "Why don't we talk about this someplace other than the middle of the laundry room? Maybe where there are comfortable chairs, and privacy?"

She sighed. "Okay, living room, den, or library?"

"Any of the above would do."

She walked out of the utility room, Mike at her heels.

Marms tagged along. He wasn't getting anywhere with Mrs. O'Malley and the roast.

As they passed through the kitchen, the cook was hanging up the phone. She turned, her face worried. "The mister told me to watch out and keep the doors locked. What's going on?"

Emma looked at Mike. She trusted both the O'Malley's implicitly. How much did the cook need to know?

Mike said, "Let's get back with you on that. For now, everything's fine. We'll be in the…" He looked at Emma. "Living room?" At her nod, he continued, "Come get me if you see anything unusual."

"All right. Dinner will be ready soon." A frown puckered her forehead. She turned her attention back to the oven to check on their meal.

As they walked past the fridge, Emma snagged a couple of sodas. Mike had passed through the adjoining rooms and locked the front door when she caught up with him. He joined her in the living room.

They sat on the couch in front of the fireplace, turning to face each other. Emma handed him a cola.

"Okay," she said, "let me get this straight. Mr. O'Malley took the brooch to Mr. Sun for repairs. Once there, the killer comes in, demands it—that's what I heard him yelling, and he was saying something about a sun, but I thought he was referring to Mr. Sun's name— and once he has it, he kills Mr. Sun."

"That's it in a nutshell," Mike agreed. "But there are other things not accounted for. Why this brooch? It's not supposed to be very pretty, although it probably has value since it's gold. And why a brooch—supposedly, Mr. Kerwood was upset when he saw what his wife had done to it and said he couldn't *use it* now. What was it before she had it made into a brooch?"

"Maybe it wasn't a piece of jewelry at all." Emma thought aloud. "A paperweight? Was it hollow? Maybe it held something else of great value." Her eyes lit up. "I know. It held diamonds or a tiny piece of paper folded up, like a treasure map."

"Well, if it did, then it would still lead him right back here and right into our laps."

Emma ignored his sarcasm. "So it can be *used* for something, and he has it, and supposedly that something is right here. Why hasn't he shown up to *use* it?"

"Maybe the house being inhabited by a young woman and friend has made him hesitate. Perhaps he's waiting until it's quiet around here. Didn't you say the donation truck had been here during the week?"

"Yeah, for two days. Seems like they were here a lot." She shrugged. "I *thought* it was quiet."

"Peaceful for you, but still too many people coming and going. However, if he gets tired of waiting, you and Tina might not be a problem after all."

"So he might just, uh…" She couldn't continue.

"Come in, shoot you, or whatever, and take what he wants." He glanced around the living room. "It would have to be something of great value."

Emma looked around as well. "There's lots of stuff here, and I'm sure some of it's pretty valuable."

"Have you been through the whole house?"

"Just the first couple of floors, really. I was on the third floor, but just a little. There's not much up there."

"Why don't we go on a grand tour of the house. This time we'll both try to look at things in a new light, like what someone might kill to get their hands on." Mike stood.

Emma sighed, then got to her feet. "Okay. But I just had a thought."

At Mike's questioning look, Emma continued, "Whatever it is he's willing to kill for, I hope I didn't give it to the charity service."

Chapter Seventeen

Joseph Malone listened on his cell phone to the man he knew only as the Buyer, and his idea of how he should wrap this up now that they had identified and found the witness. The Buyer outlined a plan whereby Joseph could set up in the deserted house behind the former Kerwood residence and wait until Emma made an appearance. He could simply take her out with a single gunshot. Joseph's face pinched in irritation as he waited until the man finished.

"It wouldn't work. There are too many risks. I don't think I would miss, but what if I did? You know the police watch out for her. They'd be swarming the place before I could escape. There's only one way in and out. I'd be trapped like a rat in a cage."

Joseph sat in his car in a crowded parking lot at a lakeside restaurant. He blended right in with the customers coming and going, but he didn't intend to stay much longer. Someone might wonder about the lone man sitting in his car chatting on his cell phone. When the Buyer called him about the witness, he was in Tulsa. Malone was able to head to Grove and check into Emma and her new location. He didn't like what he saw. That isolation provided her security.

"Well, then," continued the Buyer, "I have another idea, but it has risks, too." He began to outline an alternate plan, and Malone smiled as he listened. At least the odds were getting more even.

****

Emma started their search on the third floor. They checked the rooms quickly, as she had done earlier when she explored on her own.

She opened a large cedar chest and turned to look at Mike. "Just what *are* we looking for?" she asked.

"They say in the movies, we'll know it when we see it," he answered. He poked through an old chest of drawers. They finished looking and headed down, satisfied that whatever they were searching for wasn't there.

"A lot of stuff has been given to the donation center on this floor. We pretty well cleaned the closets out," Emma said as they wandered together into one of the back bedrooms. She opened a closet door and glanced inside at the empty interior. "We were thinking of making the second floor more livable, so we got rid of all the old people stuff." She pulled out a bureau drawer; Mike did the same across the room at a bedside table. Both were empty.

Emma placed her hands on her hips and stood to face him. "I'm afraid most of the rooms up here are going to look like this. Tina and mine will have more, but it's our own belongings."

He waved his hand toward the door. "Let's go through them anyway, so we don't feel like we're missing anything."

As they sped through the bedrooms, a thought struck him. "Is there a safe in the house?" At her blank look, he clarified, "You know, a safe to keep valuables in."

"Oh." Emma frowned as she thought. "No. I haven't seen one. That's kind of odd, isn't it? As rich as he was

162

and not have a safe?"

"We should ask Mrs. O'Malley." He glanced at his watch. "She's probably waiting dinner on us now. She said an hour, and it's past. We better get down there."

They hurried down the wide staircase, and the aroma of pot roast drifted up to them. Emma clutched her stomach as a loud growl emanated from it. Mike clutched his own a few seconds later as an even louder growl came forth.

Emma laughed at his expression. "Let's go get some dinner."

The dining table was large and set with fine china and gleaming silverware. It was designed to seat up to twelve, but the cook had arranged the seating at one end of the long table. Emma admired the pretty setting displayed for them. "God bless her. She is so sweet," she murmured when Mrs. O'Malley bustled out of the kitchen.

"Oh, there you are, just in time," the cook said. She shooed them toward their seats. "The mister is not much for it, but I talked him into helping me serve you. Bless him. He's more comfortable outside in the dirt and the grass than in a proper dining room. Sit, sit!" They scurried like children toward their seats. The older woman hustled along in their wake.

"Mrs. O'Malley, you really don't have to do all this. We can wait on ourselves," Emma protested as Mike held her chair for her. "It was enough that you cooked such a super meal."

"Oh nonsense, I enjoyed myself. I haven't had much chance to cook lately, and I love it." She beamed at Emma and Mike, happy and anxious to have them enjoy the food. Emma saw movement behind the cook, and she leaned to see Mr. O'Malley as he balanced a large platter of pot roast. He slowly made his way out of the kitchen.

Emma smiled. He tried to pull off the part of butler, but his weather-roughened countenance, overalls, and flannel shirt did not suit. Mike followed her gaze, and his face split into a wide grin. Mrs. O'Malley looked behind her to see why they were smiling. She shrieked at her husband.

"Be careful!"

"Now, missus, I've got it, and I fully intend to make it to the table without dropping this."

"Marms, you scoot!" The cat's eyes had grown big at the sight of the meat. He moved forward, his tail flagstaff high. He avoided Mr. O'Malley's booted foot and moved back to safer ground. His gaze never left the food platter.

Mrs. O'Malley returned to the kitchen, then hurried back armed with a casserole dish of seasoned new potatoes. She sent Mr. O'Malley back for another plate of vegetables and freshly baked bread. By the time all the food was in place, Emma knew there was no way the two of them could finish it. She looked at Mike, her eyes inquiring. He nodded.

"Mr. And Mrs. O'Malley, would you please join us? Emma asked. "You've worked so hard, and there is so much food. We really would like for you to eat with us."

The cook opened her mouth to decline when her husband intercepted her.

"Don't mind if we do," he burst out and turned to the large hutch in the room and gathered matching plates for him and his wife. Mrs. O'Malley stood red-faced and glared at him as he put a plate down for her and pulled out a chair next to Emma. "Have a seat, missus. Emma's been good enough to invite us to sit down with them and share a meal, and I think that's very polite and nice of her. We all know how hard you've worked cooking this meal. You should enjoy it too."

He looked at Emma quickly, wondering if he had gone too far. After all, his wife had been on the payroll while she made this meal, but at Emma's wide smile, he knew she wasn't taking any offense.

At her husband's direction, Mrs. O'Malley sat next to Emma. She looked flushed and uncomfortable, so Emma reached over and patted her hand to put her at ease.

"I think this meal looks and smells great, and Mr. O'Malley did the right thing to accept my invitation and enjoy it with us." As the older woman looked a little more at ease, Emma continued, "Besides, there's way too much food for just Mike and me."

Mr. O'Malley returned with the utensils, and Mike poured them all a glass of red wine. Emma said the prayer. Then, all went quiet as they dug into their meal.

****

As they finished eating, Mike announced he had never had such a delicious meal.

"That's because the missus here is one of the best cooks in the county," Mr. O'Malley said. He pulled a toothpick and stuck it between his teeth. "I don't pretend to know anything about fixing food and would starve if I had to depend on my own cooking. But the missus," he nodded affectionately across the table at his wife, "she can cook anything, and it tastes wonderful. She's never burned a thing."

Mrs. O'Malley smiled in a secret sort of way. "The mister has more of a selective memory as he gets older.

But I don't mind. I'll take all the compliments I can get."

This opened for Mike and Emma to exclaim about how good the food was and ended with Mrs. O'Malley waving her hands and telling them to "Shush."

"I wasn't fishing for compliments. I wasn't!" She beamed at them. "But I'm very glad you enjoyed it, and there's apple pie for dessert."

Mike groaned and leaned back in his chair.

Emma spoke for both. "I'd like to wait until later for that if you don't mind. Apple pie sounds perfect, but more so, two hours from now. Would you mind? But if you want some, please go ahead. We can help ourselves later."

Emma remembered they had been in the middle of searching the house for the purpose of the brooch when they had been interrupted to sit down and eat.

"Mrs. O'Malley," she said, "Did Mr. Kerwood have a safe?"

The woman looked a little surprised at the question. "That's not something Mr. Kerwood would have normally shared with me, or the mister, Miss Emma. We were pretty close to him, and he trusted us. He was a good employer, but he never took us into his confidence as to a safe."

"In all your cleaning, you never noticed one?"

Mrs. O'Malley shook her head. "No, miss, I didn't."

"Did he have a room that he would specifically keep you out of? Didn't want you cleaning thoroughly or wanted you to stay out of it if he were in there?"

Mrs. O'Malley wrinkled her forehead as she thought. "He didn't want me in his bedroom much, but I just assumed that was because he wanted his privacy. Sometimes, he would tell me to leave the library alone.

'I'm busy, I don't want to be disturbed,' he would say."

"His bedroom?" Emma asked. "His original one upstairs or downstairs?"

"Downstairs."

Emma looked at Mr. O'Malley, and he shook his head. "I never did much inside the house. Maybe fix something once in a while. I never saw a safe."

"Okay." Emma thought aloud. "Do you know what he did in the library?"

"No, Miss Emma, I have no idea." She stood and cast a meaningful look at Mr. O'Malley. "Well, if you want to wait on pie, I think we need to be cleaning up these dishes, so we can enjoy that pie later. Mister, would you like to help me?"

"O'course." He shuffled plates together to carry into the kitchen.

Emma looked at Mike as he slid his chair back to leave the table. "They've never seen a safe. So, I assume if there is one, it's hidden."

"I would say most definitely hidden, and I would bet there is one," he said as he helped her move her chair.

They walked out of the room together. "The bedroom or the library?" she asked. "I bet the library."

"I agree," he answered as they left the dining room.

In the foyer, Marms sat statue stiff, only his tail twitched. Emma stopped, reached over, and touched Mike's arm.

Chapter Eighteen

Mike's gaze followed hers to the big cat. The feline sat, tail waved slowly, just outside the living room. His attention was focused on something within the room. Something, Mike guessed, Marms did not like.

Their movement caught the cat's attention, and he glanced at them, then resumed his stare into the living room.

Emma hesitated, then remembered, *this is my house*, and pushed forward. Mike reached out to grab her arm, but she was already out of his reach. As he caught up with her, she was at the double doors to the living room and entered it.

Sitting on the couch as though it was hers was Nancy Karroll. Dressed in a black and gray outfit, with perfectly matching low-heeled shoes, she sat sideways, her back toward the door, chatting with a tall, fair-haired man beside her. He was also very relaxed, as though he belonged there.

What gives? Emma advanced toward them, Mike behind her.

"Miss Karroll?" she asked. The nurse swung around and faced her, an automatic smile plastered in place as she looked at Emma. "What are you doing here?"

The nurse stood, as did the man beside her. "Miss Stone!" She exclaimed, stepping toward Emma. She stretched out her hand. "My brother came to visit me, and

I wanted him to meet you."

Emma slowly took the outstretched hand but frowned at Nancy Karroll. "How did you get in here? Who let you in?"

"The door was open, so we came in." She continued to smile broadly at Emma, who glanced back at Mike. "I'm sorry, should we have waited? I'm so used to coming and going in this house, I just didn't think about it, so we just came on in and sat down to wait for you." She looked apologetic as she added, "We could smell food, so assumed we might have arrived while you were eating and didn't want to bother you."

As Emma continued to look at her as though she didn't believe a word she said, Nancy looked over at her brother. "Maybe we should leave. Another time might be better." As he nodded in agreement, Emma shook her head.

"No, that's okay. You just caught me by surprise, that's all. Of course, you're welcome. I would imagine it's hard to get used to thinking you shouldn't walk right in as you're used to doing." *Was this intrusion unintentional? I must tell her she's no longer free to come and go into the house as before. Wait a minute. She knocked at the door earlier. What's different now? And Mike locked the door earlier before we searched the house.*

Distracted by her thoughts, Emma was brought back to reality by the nurse's voice.

"This is Ernest, my brother. He's visiting for a few days, and I was hoping to show him around a bit." Nancy Karroll beamed as she introduced him.

Emma went through the automatic polite motions, shaking his hand, uttering niceties, then turned to introduce Mike. "This is Mike, he's…"

Before Emma could continue, Mike grasped the outstretched hand of Ernest Karroll. "I'm a friend of Emma's. From Tulsa. Pleased to meet you." Standing close to Emma, he nudged her in the side with his elbow.

Emma smiled, remembering her conversation earlier with Ms. Karroll. "So you see, Ms. Karroll, I do have friends from Tulsa who visit me here in the wilds of Grove."

Nancy Karroll looked a little uncomfortable, but it was instantly gone. "I guess I was a little hasty in thinking you were too far from your friends." She smiled at Emma and turned to sit back down on the couch, followed by her brother. Both then looked up at Emma expectantly.

"Can I get you something? Drinks?" Emma asked, trying to maintain politeness. They were certainly pushing her good manner buttons. She wanted to tell them to leave and come back another time, but she felt they expected her to cater to them as guests. She would go along with it for a bit, but her patience was short. She didn't want to waste the precious time she had with her other guest. She was surprised to see Mike studying the couple. He wore a slight frown.

"Mrs. O'Malley used to make the most delicious, sweet tea. Would you happen to have some of that on hand? I've told my brother she makes the best." Nancy smiled, showing lots of teeth, a smile Emma was quickly learning to hate.

"Yes. There's some in the fridge. I'll get it. Mike?" He followed her to the door, keeping the Karrolls in his side vision. Just outside the doors, they stopped.

"Go get the tea. I'll stay here. Someone needs to

keep an eye on them. Wonder how long they were in there?"

"I don't know. I never heard the door or anything." She headed toward the kitchen, then turned around.

"Mike, if anyone knows where a safe might be, it could be her. Do you think that's why they snuck in?"

"The thought crossed my mind."

Mike returned to the living room as Emma hurried to the kitchen. There, she ran into the O'Malleys and told them about the Karrolls's surprise visit.

They both talked at once and over each other. "Miss Emma, you be careful around them."

"Don't tell them anything you don't have to. And get them out of here as soon as you can."

Emma returned with the tea to find Mike by the fireplace, chatting with the Karrolls. They all looked relieved to see her approach, and she surmised the conversation was not an easy one. Mike probably wanted to ask more pointed questions but held back since he was also, technically, a guest. But she could. The fact that they just walked into her house still rankled.

Setting the tray loaded with iced tea on the coffee table, Emma handed each a glass. She sat down on the opposite couch and said, "Now tell me again, *why* are you here?"

Ms. Karroll took a sip of her tea and gave a delicate lick to her lips. "Ahh, that's so good." She addressed Emma. "I was hoping you would give my brother a tour of the estate. He's only going to be here a short while, and I didn't think it would take very long."

Emma considered it. On the one hand, she resented Ms. Karroll and her brother and their obvious intrusion. On other hand, the woman might know something that would be beneficial for them. She glanced at Mike, whose attention had been caught by something to the side of her intrusive guests. A slight smile crept across his lips.

Following the direction of his gaze, Emma saw Marms, twitched and prepared to pounce on Nancy Karroll. Emma knew that look. Like most felines, Marms knew instinctively which people did not like cats, and those people were like magnets to him. Emma sprang to catch him, shouting, "Marms, no!" as the big cat made a jump onto the couch. Emma's leap caused him to land behind the woman rather than on her lap as intended.

There was a moment of confusion and noise as Emma grabbed Marms and Nancy Karroll squealed. She moved around to avoid the cat and spilled her tea. Marms tried to wiggle out of Emma's grasp, but she had done this before and had a firm grip on his furry body.

Ernest's eyes were wide with surprise. He grabbed his tea with both hands to avoid spilling it. Nancy put hers down on the tray and glared at Emma, the large cat still squirming in her arms. Emma glanced over at Mike, who, by the twist of his lips, was having a difficult time keeping his laughter under control.

"I *am* sorry," Emma apologized. She sat, her arms still locked around Marms. His attention never wavered from the Karrolls. Emma situated the big cat on her lap, rubbing his head affectionately. "He's usually better behaved than this."

Nancy Karroll apparently saw Marms's bad behavior as a way to get Emma to give them a tour. "Maybe if you will just give my brother a quick look at the estate, we can go on about our business, and we'll be out of your hair, so to speak."

Emma frowned. What was so important about this estate that she wanted her brother to have a tour so badly? Ernest had hardly spoken a word. He'd let his sister do all the talking.

Emma looked directly at Ernest. "Why?" she asked him point blank. "Why do you want a tour? It's just a big house on pretty land. And I live here. It's not like the place is set up with a tour guide. And haven't you been here before?"

He had the decency to look embarrassed. "Nancy," he said to his sister, glancing over at Emma, "this is obviously not a good time, and we've disturbed Emma and her other guest. I think we should leave." And to Emma's last question, he added, "Yes, I've been here before, but this is the first time I've been inside the house. Mr. Kerwood was not very, um, approachable."

He took a final drink of his tea and placed it on the tray beside Nancy's. "Thank you very much for the tea, and we're sorry to have bothered you." He rose to leave, Nancy rising to go beside him.

His conciliatory manner caused a wave of guilt to pass over Emma. She glanced at Mike, who looked at the floor, leaving the question up to her. She sighed and pushed Marms off to the side. He settled; his tail brushed across Emma's arm. "Okay. We'll do a quick look." At Ernest Karroll's sudden look of pleasure, she added, "But I don't know much about the history of the place."

Standing, she pointed to the front entry. "Let's start at the entrance."

They all trooped out of the room, and Emma led the way. "This is the entrance hall, that's the grand staircase…"

Mike took up the rear, and Marms trotted along

behind him. He bent and picked up the cat. "I think it's up to us to keep an eye on these two, don't you agree, fella?" Marms purred in agreement.

****

The so-called tour was, as Emma had indicated, quick. She walked her guests through the house at a fast pace, Ernest making the appropriate noises of appreciation, Nancy glancing around as though it was all new to her. They lingered in the library the longest. Nancy and Ernest remarked on the large number of books in Mr. Kerwood's collection.

Emma commented on the unusual scenic bronze wall plate. "I think it's just different from other items Mr. Kerwood displayed in his house."

Neither Ernest nor Nancy seemed particularly interested in it.

Having completed the tour inside, they stepped outside. Clouds had gathered, and a light rain misted.

Ernest turned to Emma and held out his hand. "I think we can forgo seeing the grounds at this time, Ms. Stone. I appreciate you taking time to show me around. It's a beautiful place." Emma shook his hand, and he turned to go. His sister was already at her car door.

As they drove away, Emma turned to Mike. "Well, whatever they wanted to see, they saw, and they're ready to go. Did they find what they were looking for? Maybe he really *did* want to see the place before his visit was over. What do you think?"

Mike shook his head. "I don't think so. But I've been wondering if they're either one, in any way, connected with Mr. Sun's murder and the robbery."

"Ernest doesn't look like Joseph Malone. And I don't see how Nancy could be connected."

"I know." He looked down at Marms. The cat sat and watched the Karrolls drive off, his tail still moving. He stood and trotted through the open doors into the house. "Marms certainly didn't like them," Mike added.

Emma turned to follow his gaze in time to see the big cat's bottlebrush tail disappear inside the house. "Marms has been a pretty good indicator of how much I should trust people." She smiled, remembering back to when Mike had first met the big cat. "*You*, I should trust. But them, *no*."

He slipped an arm around her and gave her a quick squeeze. "Smart cat you have there, Ms. Stone."

Another thought came to her. "Mike, you *did* lock the front door earlier, didn't you?"

"Yes. So, when Nancy said the front door was open, she lied. She still has a key. You haven't changed the locks yet, have you?"

"No. Didn't see a need to."

They stood for a moment, looking down the long, shaded driveway to the house. They watched the Karroll vehicle disappear. Emma felt a brief chill, and she knew it wasn't the cool breeze.

"Mike," she said, looking up at him, her brow in a slight frown. He looked down, eyebrows raised.

"What?"

"Don't take this wrong, and I know I have no right to ask…" Emma was obviously uncomfortable with her line of thought.

Mike found her enchanting. "What?" he asked again.

"I know it's your day off, and you probably have other things to do, and oh my gosh, you probably have a girlfriend to get back to…" Her mouth was speaking as her thoughts formed.

He chuckled. "So if I have a girlfriend, why am I standing here with my arm around you, and why did I kiss you earlier and thoroughly enjoy it, I might add?"

"Oh." Emma blushed, feeling more uncomfortable by the second. She broke away from him, fanning her face with her hand, hoping to make the embarrassing blush go away. It seemed in no hurry to fade, so she decided to jump right in.

"Would it be too much of an inconvenience for you to spend the night? Here? We have lots of bedrooms, as you know, and they have beds in them, and I'd be glad to make up one for you, and you can leave as early as you want in the morning. I haven't been alone in this house yet, and Tina's gone, and you know. Joseph Malone might break in, wanting to do something with that brooch that I'm beginning to hate."

He put a finger on her lips. She quieted, her eyes large and hopeful on his face. She took off again. "I just don't want you to think that I'm thinking anything sexual, as I'm not that kind of girl." She rolled her eyes at that last statement as she realized that sounded like something her mother would say. She groaned, her face red with embarrassment.

Mike laughed out loud and pulled her against him. She tucked her forehead against his chest, trying to hide her red face. He dropped a quick kiss on top of her head.

"No problem. I'm off tomorrow, and I'd be glad to stay the night. I'd consider it my duty to keep my favorite witness safe."

Emma pulled back a little so she could see his face. "Just your duty?"

Mike delivered a kiss to her forehead, then one on

each cheek as he raised his hands to cup her face. She tilted her face, her eyes closed, inviting. Before his lips touched hers, he whispered, "It's all pleasure."

Chapter Nineteen

After Mike agreed to spend the night, they decided it should appear he had left. He would drive his car into town and leave it. Emma would go to town later, and they would return and slip into the house after nightfall.

They sat on the iron bench at the edge of the front porch, talking quietly for an hour. Mike rose to leave and gave Emma a long kiss, with a look that said he didn't want to leave. She gave him a playful push and said, "You better go now. It's a long drive back. I can't wait until next weekend."

He drove off and waved one last time. Emma returned his wave with a lingering sadness in her eyes.

With a little shrug and grin, she turned to go back into the house. *That went well, I hope.* A secretive little smile caressed her lips.

With her purse on her shoulder and shopping list in hand, Emma left the house. She portrayed the average American woman bent on a quick shopping trip to a local discount store.

She met Mike at the shop, made some quick purchases, and they returned to the estate in Emma's car. She parked in the multi-car garage adjacent to the barn where Mr. O'Malley kept his landscaping equipment.

Darkness had fallen. Emma had purposely left all outside lights off earlier. Inside the garage, Mike eased out the side door and slipped across the lawn in the dark.

Using a key Emma gave him, he entered the house through the back door. Emma made the more obvious entrance through the front to appear as if she returned alone from her shopping trip. A sack full of merchandise swung from her arm.

She entered the silent, dark house. *If I didn't know Mike was here, this would feel creepy.* Emma turned on the lights, and the large chandelier gave her a warm welcome. Glancing around the huge hall, she didn't see anyone lurking in the corner with a gun pointed at her. She let out a sigh of relief.

She walked quietly over to the dining room. In a stage whisper, she called out, "Mike?"

"I'm here," he responded, so close that she jumped. She reached for the light switch to flip it on, but he stopped her. "Leave the light out in this room. Those big patio doors would light us up to anyone outside."

"But we don't really *know* if anyone is watching, do we? What are we going to do if no one *is* watching? How long is this going to go on?" Emma's whispers rose in pitch.

Mike took her hand and led her to the den, the room that Mr. Kerwood had remodeled into his bedroom, and then Emma had changed back to a den by removing the bedroom furniture. It was the most secluded room downstairs.

Emma slung her sacks onto the tan couch and bounced into a corner of the sofa. She frowned at Mike.

"I don't like waiting for something to happen and not knowing when or even *what* is going to happen." She heaved a sigh and settled on the couch more comfortably.

Mike sat on the other end of the couch. "You wouldn't like a stake out very much then. Sometimes, you wait hours, days, or even weeks for something to happen. When it does, it's usually quick."

"Good thing that's not what I do. What *do* you think will happen? And when?"

"I think Joseph Malone will come here to do something with that brooch. Whatever that brooch is supposed to do. But the connection is *here*, so I think the estate is where he's going to come."

"So, you think he'll come tonight?"

"I don't know. But it's possible."

"So okay, you're here now, so if he comes tonight, I feel that we'll take care of him." Mike frowned at the term *we*, but Emma ignored him and continued. "But what about tomorrow night or anytime later? You can't stay here all the time, not without proof that he's about to come back. I know you have other cases that need your attention."

"I think, knowing what we know now, that the police can spare a man to sit out front on a twenty-four-hour watch. They'd love to catch a high-priority thief like Joseph Malone." Mike looked satisfied with his answer, but Emma was having none of it.

"So, he's patient. He'll wait us out. The police chief will get tired of wasting a man here twenty-four hours a day and will put him back on regular duty. Then he shows up, and I don't have a clue how to defend myself against him." She looked at the floor and frowned. "Nor do I want to. I don't want to think about how to fight someone. I don't want to live my life in that kind of fear. Can we flush him out, set a trap like they do on TV or in the movies?"

"That's what we're doing right now. We just didn't intend it that way." At Emma's puzzled look, he continued, "Everybody's gone. You're here alone, at your most vulnerable. If he's around, *now* is the best time for him to make his move."

Emma sighed heavily and pushed a stray lock of hair behind her ear. "You're right. It's just hard to realize what danger we might be sitting in right now, just waiting for something to happen." She paused, then continued, "You know, I lead a quiet life, really, I do. I never asked for much excitement or danger. I *like* my life. But maybe I was getting complacent, taking things for granted. Hearing Mr. Sun pleading for his life, and that gunshot that killed him, and all *this*..." She waved her arms wide to encompass the house. "*This* has almost been too much for quiet little me. I want to get this all over with, catch Malone, return to normal."

She looked at Mike and continued sadly, "Then I realize how selfish I am. I am at least alive, and maybe I can help in catching Malone. Mr. Sun's family will have to live without him."

Readjusting her position on the couch, legs up in front of her and arms wrapped around them, she turned and faced Mike. "So. Do you really think he's out there right now, waiting for, what? To get late enough? Me to go to bed? All the lights to go out?" She looked pointedly at the gun in his shoulder holster. Mike had slipped it on after he left the house earlier. "Do you really think you'll need to use that?"

"I hope not," he answered. "But if Malone shows up, I'll need it, because I'm sure he'll come armed."

****

Emma looked at the wall clock. Almost nine o'clock. The last few hours had slipped by quickly, but she felt time would drag on now. "What should we do?

181

Just sit here? Watch some TV? Act like a normal night?"

"Yes, I think you should act as though this were a regular evening. I'll stay out of sight and keep watch."

"You can't stay up all night."

"I'll worry about that when I start getting sleepy. You've got plenty of coffee?"

"Of course."

"What would you normally be doing about this time? If he has an eye on you, he'll be watching for your usual behavior."

Emma shrugged. "I don't know. Watch some TV, and maybe Tina and I would have gone out to a movie, dinner. We haven't started a pattern yet, and remember, this *is* the first time I've been here alone and at night."

"So if you were home in Tulsa, what would you do?"

"Probably go out with friends. Maybe have a date." She gave him a flirty blink at the last suggestion.

Mike grinned. "How 'bout we pretend this is a date, and we'll stay home instead of dressing up and going somewhere? A quiet evening at home? Got any movies?"

"I've got movie channels and cable. And this is the best TV in the house right here."

"Sounds good." He settled more comfortably on the couch, raised the recliner portion, and looked pointedly at the large screen TV in front of them. Emma sighed, retrieved the remote, and flipped on the set. She muted it and asked, "So how long are we going to watch TV?"

"Just until it gets a little later. Then you'll go on to bed, and I'll check the house."

"Okay." She sat, and he pulled her against his side. She didn't object and snuggled against him, her legs tucked up on the seat. "So how much of a pretend date is this?"

"Well, I don't want to get too distracted in case we hear something. If we were on a real date, I would be distracted." He smiled and winked at her. "Let's just watch a movie for now. What's on?"

They agreed on an old classic movie. About halfway into the show, Mike announced that he was going to make a quick sweep of the house and would return.

While he was gone, Emma decided drinks and popcorn would be good. She passed the central staircase on her way to the kitchen.

Marms lay curled on the bottom step, his front paws dangling. She stopped to rub him. He stretched and sat up, yawned wide. His sharp little teeth were displayed.

"What are you doing here?" she asked. "You never sit on the stairs." He rubbed his head against her hand, and she left him to go to the kitchen.

In the den, Emma sat down the two colas and a large bowl of popcorn. Mike entered and announced, "All is quiet outside."

They settled back down, sipped cola, and munched popcorn.

The movie was over. They talked for a few minutes about how they each liked that era and the shows that came from it.

"Okay. It's late, and I'm turning in," Emma announced quietly. She went from room to room and extinguished lights as she passed through. She stopped at the foot of the staircase and looked up at Mike, standing next to her. Only a dim night light provided any visual. She leaned against him and whispered, "Goodnight kiss?"

He didn't hesitate but leaned down and kissed her

softly. He pulled back to see her still leaning toward him, eyes closed, a soft smile across her lips.

"Oh, what the heck," he murmured and pulled her close. He wrapped his arms around her waist for a longer, deeper kiss. Her hands curled around his neck, and she snuggled up to him, thoroughly enjoying his masculine scent and taste. When he ended the kiss and pushed her gently back, it was with regret. "Go to bed. I'll see you in the morning."

A quick little kiss in the air and Emma strolled to the staircase, where once again Marms was settled on the bottom step. She gathered up the big cat and held him across her shoulder like a baby. He didn't mind, instead rubbing his head alongside her neck. He was used to being cuddled this way.

Emma climbed the stairs slower because of the twenty pounds of cat she carried. She lowered Marms to the floor and opened the door to her room. Marms looked in for a second before he followed her. In the bedroom, she noticed Marms again waiting outside the door, giving the room the once-over before he entered.

In her bedroom, Emma sat in the chair and removed her shoes. She watched Marms jump on the bed, turn a circle, and flop down. He blinked at her as she talked to him.

"What's up with you? You're usually Mister-Open-The-Door-For-Me-and-Move-Out-Of-My-Way-So-I-Can-Get-In-First cat. Is something wrong?" Emma glanced around the room. Nothing seemed out of place.

She headed toward the bathroom to brush her teeth and wash her face, rubbing Marms's head as she passed by. He rolled over to watch her.

Emma came out of the bathroom, intent on getting a

nightgown.

At the closet door, Marms stood on his hind legs to scratch the wood frame, using both paws. Emma stopped and watched him.

What could be in there? Mice? She snorted. *Like any mouse would dare live in a place where Mrs. O'Malley was in charge.* She reached for the doorknob, and Marms stuck his nose even closer to the door. Emma nudged him aside with her foot. "Move back," she ordered as she turned the knob.

The door slammed open with enough force to knock Emma backward and hard to the floor. Her head bounced against the side of the bed. When her vision cleared, Joseph Malone stood over her, pointing the largest handgun she'd ever seen at her face.

"Oh," she managed to breathe. He held the gun before him. It did not waver. The man was larger than she remembered and more frightening.

"What do you want?" she whispered. She managed to look from the gun to his eyes. They were mere slits of fury.

Not one to waste time with small talk, Malone held out a pair of handcuffs. "Put these on," he instructed, his voice deep and gravelly. "One on the right wrist, the other around that bedpost." Not taking his gaze off her, he nodded to the end of her bed.

Still wobbly from the impact, Emma struggled to her feet and did as instructed. She fastened the handcuff to her wrist, then looked at the bedpost as if she had never seen it before. Indeed, she never imagined it as a manacle post. It resembled a spire, almost to the ceiling. There was a narrow area in the middle where the handcuff could fit. As she fastened the metal around it, Malone moved with lightning speed. He picked her legs up and dropped her on the bed. He produced a roll of tape and efficiently wrapped it tightly around her ankles.

At this point, Emma realized she needed to make some noise. She sucked in a big breath, but Malone was ready for that, too. He quickly stuffed one of her own socks into her mouth.

A range of emotions flowed through Emma. Scared, physically hurt, and now angry. *Really, you went through my sock drawer?*

"Hold still." He pulled the tape out again and bent over Emma. She tried shaking her head from side to side to elude him but was unsuccessful. She soon had a tight piece of tape stretched across her mouth and around her head. Malone reached for her free hand, and Emma slapped at him. He snarled, but his reflexes were fast. He grabbed her hand and used the tape to bind her wrists together, so she had no freedom of movement and was latched securely to the bedpost.

Malone stood back and pulled a cell phone from his pocket. Emma sat awkwardly on the bed, her hands raised in the air, latched to the bedpost, her ankles wrapped together and a sock in her mouth. Totally helpless, she watched Malone talk quietly on the phone, then hang up. Her eyes were wide and shiny, her heart beat frantically as she wondered what he was going to do with her. What would he do to Mike when he found him downstairs?

Malone looked at her as he spoke. "*You* are a lucky young woman. And I hope never to see you again." He shouldered his gun, spun on his heels, and walked out of the room.

Chapter Twenty

The outside check of the house complete, Mike headed inside when two vehicles drove up and parked. He watched from the shadows as the front door of the house opened, and Joseph Malone stepped out.

Should I call the police or wait? He decided to wait and see who exited, as Malone, by his offhand manner, expected the drivers.

Nancy Karroll and her brother got out of the cars and jogged up the steps toward Malone. Mike swung around the corner of the house and made a quick call to the local police. He told the dispatcher Malone was there, armed, and he had company.

Malone stood a couple of feet from him, his gun against Mike's right temple. "I'll take this, detective," he said as he reached with his other hand and took Mike's gun. He turned back to the Karrolls, who stood open-jawed and staring. "The police will be here any minute, hurry!"

His urgency prompted them to action, and they ran into the house, stumbling across Marms, who'd followed Malone down the stairs. Ernest kicked him out of the way. They hurried into the library.

"Sorry about this, chap," Malone said. Before Mike turned to see what he meant, Malone slammed the butt of his gun against Mike's head. He collapsed in a heap on the floor.

With Mike out of the way, Malone stopped outside the library door and addressed the couple. "I'm out of here. I've done my job."

The two were obsessed with the brooch. They turned it back and forth, passing it between them. He considered interrupting them, but it was precious seconds he couldn't spare.

Running out of the house, he jumped in the first car and peeled out. His goal was to make it to the highway before the police caught him. At a Texas airport, a private plane waited for him.

****

Nancy and Ernest bickered over the brooch, standing before the large bronze winter scene that was embedded in the wall of the library. Nancy was trying to force it into the recessed area where the sun was in the picture. It wasn't cooperating.

"Can't you see it doesn't go in like that? You can't turn it with those long nails of yours!" Ernest argued as she tried to wiggle it in place.

"Okay, then you do it. We don't have much time." Nancy let go of the brooch, and it crashed on the shelf below.

Ernest scooped it up. "Let me try."

He forced the brooch into the indentation and pushed hard until he heard a click. There was a metallic whirr. Nothing further happened. He pushed a second time. After an additional metallic whine, the entire motif swung outward. A dial was exposed.

Ernest glanced at his sister. "What's the combination?"

The look on his sister's face told him she had no clue. He shouted at her. "Dammit, Nancy! How could you let us get this far and not know the combination?" He ran his hand through his sparse blond hair and glared at her. "We don't have time for this. The police will be here any minute. Think!"

Nancy licked her lips. "Try his birthday, 2-25-12."

Ernest turned the combination carefully. There was a tremendous crash overhead, and the wall shook. Nancy looked at him, but he didn't waste a second.

"See what that was. We don't want anything else coming to stop us." As she hesitated, he looked at her and yelled, "Go!"

Nancy flew out of the room and glanced up the stairs. Nothing looked out of place. She ran as fast as she could up the staircase. Seeing a bedroom light to her right, she slowed down and approached carefully, peeking around the open door.

A huge beam of wood barreled out of the bedroom directly at her. The former bedpost punched her hard in the stomach and knocked the breath out of her. Before Nancy lost consciousness, she caught a glimpse of Emma behind the wooden post, her hair wild around her face. She had an angry welt across her mouth, duct tape hanging loose around her neck, and a fierce look in her eyes. "I don't *like* being a prisoner in my own home. Remember that!"

Glaring at Nancy lying on the floor, Emma didn't know why the woman was there, but she was angry at anyone who got in her way now. She knew somehow Nancy was involved in her predicament. She dragged the bedpost to the staircase and moved down as quickly as possible. She figured the bed would never be the same, and she didn't care. Her hands were still taped together, but she'd managed to grab the tape and sock and free up her mouth. With a few more gymnastic moves, she had removed the tape around her ankles as well.

The bedpost bumped on each step as she moved downstairs. *So much for sneaking up on someone.* She bounced down one step at a time. Since being quiet was not an option if she wanted to keep moving, she decided she might as well make more noise.

"Mike?" she yelled out.

"In the library."

Immediate relief flooded her. *At least he's alive and sounds okay.*

What seemed like an hour later, she finished dragging the bedpost down the stairs and turned toward the library. She passed through the entry hall toward the library door. Mike leaned against the doorframe, hair mussed, gun in hand, and trained on someone inside the room.

His backup, Marms, sat at his feet, his gaze intent on the person Mike had his gun on.

As Emma approached the room, Mike risked a glance away from Ernest to see if she was all right. Seeing her lumbering along, dragging the bedpost, his glance was longer than intended.

Ernest seized the opportunity and leaped on Mike. His attention on the detective, he didn't notice Marms in his way. His foot made solid contact with the cat, who let out a yowl and hiss. This was the second time Ernest's foot had kicked the feline, and Marms didn't take it well. The large and now angry cat attacked Ernest with a vengeance, leaping against him and causing him to lose his balance.

Mike stepped back and raised his gun out of the way of the attempted safe cracker. He watched as Ernest slid across the floor and collided with a decorative table against the opposite wall. The vase on the table wobbled and crashed down on Ernest's head. He was unconscious.

Mike stared at Emma with her wooden post and Ernest's limp body. "What on earth?"

A commotion at the front door grabbed their attention as the Grove police burst into the house.

****

Among the officers crashing through the front door was the police chief, who recognized Emma immediately. When Emma stated there was another woman upstairs to be apprehended, he motioned two officers to take care of Nancy Karroll. He then turned his attention to Emma and her attached bedpost.

"How did this happen?" he asked. He pulled out his keys to remove the cuffs holding her to the beam.

"Joseph Malone," she said. "He forced me to handcuff myself to the post while he held a gun on me." She looked at Mike, her thoughts suddenly diverted back to Malone. "Did you catch him?"

"No," Mike answered. "I hate to admit he got the jump on me and knocked me out." He turned to the chief. "But not before I saw the car he left in. About a 2015 sedan, white. I didn't see the back tag, but the front advertised the Grove Auto Ranch. I'd guess he's headed for an international airport."

The chief got the handcuffs unlocked, then turned his attention to call in the information to dispatch to locate and arrest Malone. Mike produced a small pocketknife and cut the tape across Emma's wrists.

"Your wrists look terrible," he commented as he cut, then pulled the heavy tape free. Red and swollen from the tape, Mike rubbed her arms gently. "Are you okay?"

She nodded. Emma had attacked the post repeatedly with her full body weight until she succeeded to break it free from the bed. *This will hurt, but I must do it. I need to get free and help Mike.* That was the thought that kept going through her mind at the time.

When the post finally broke and crashed to the floor, it was a hard landing. Emma considered she was lucky there were no broken bones.

Ernest had regained consciousness, and Nancy was being marched down the stairs. Emma stared at both and realized she didn't have a clue what was going on. She looked at Mike, questions all over her face.

"What are they doing here?" she asked him.

Mike had a thoughtful look as he addressed both Emma and the chief. "I believe we'll find they were the masterminds, if you'll pardon the expression, as I don't think they were very smart after all."

The chief turned to his officers with a curt, "Read them their rights, and take them away." He followed Mike and Emma as Mike led them into the library.

"When I came to, Malone had conveniently laid my gun down. I grabbed it up, and I could hear Ernest cursing in here, so this is where I headed." He picked up the gold brooch that had been the object of so much attention and handed it to Emma. "I found him with this"—he nodded at the brooch—"forcing it into *that.*" This time, he nodded to the bronze plaque.

Emma looked at the brooch. They had discussed it so much, and now she cradled it in her hands. *It is quite ugly and heavy.* She looked at the wall plaque. The door had swung slightly open when Ernest worked with it, but as time passed, it had reverted to a closed position. Once again, it resembled a wall motif.

"So, this bronze thing is a safe? That would explain why we never found one. I wonder how it works." She walked over to the plaque and studied it.

"You want me to bring Karroll back in here?" the chief asked. "We can make him tell us how it works."

"No," Mike said. "He was still trying to open it when I caught him. Push the brooch in where the sun is," he said to Emma.

Emma placed it over the recessed sun. It fit perfectly. A faint *click* sounded.

"Push it again, harder," Mike said.

Emma pushed. It went in further, and a second faint *click* was heard. There was a mechanical *whirr,* and the door opened further to reveal a combination lock.

"That's it," Mike exclaimed. "He was trying to figure out the combination when I caught him."

"I wonder what he tried?" Emma thought aloud. "Obviously, it didn't work."

A commotion at the door caused them to turn to look. Mr. and Mrs. O'Malley stood there in their nightclothes, concern, confusion, and a little anger on their faces. An officer led them inside.

"Sir," the officer spoke. "They insisted on coming in. Said they had to make sure everything was all right." He looked back at the O'Malleys, offended that they, officers of the law, could not make everything all right. He nodded toward Mr. O'Malley. "He was armed, but he turned his weapon over right away."

Mrs. O'Malley jumped in as soon as the officer stopped talking. "We could see all the lights on and could see the police car lights shinin' around the house. We were worried about Miss Emma here by herself and thought we better take a look."

Emma smiled at the O'Malleys. "I appreciate you guys so much, but I'm fine."

The police chief waved his hand to dismiss his officer. "It's okay. The O'Malleys live here." To the couple, he said, "If you could've seen that beam she was waving about before we got here, you wouldn't worry about Miss Stone taking care of herself."

The chief told the O'Malleys what had happened that evening. Emma removed the brooch and held it out for them to see as the chief wound up the story.

"Yep, that's the thing Mr. Kerwood had me drop off at the jewelry store," Mr. O'Malley said as he inspected it. "Mr. Sun did a fine job puttin' it back the way it was."

He handed it back to Emma. Once again, the motif had returned to its original configuration. She placed the sun in the plaque and pushed it in twice, causing the mechanism to click and whirr again and reveal the dial. She turned to the couple.

"Mister and Mrs. O'Malley, you knew Mr. Kerwood as well as anyone. What do you think his combination might have been, assuming he got to choose the numbers?"

The O'Malleys looked at each other for a few seconds, then Mrs. O'Malley turned to Emma and said with certainty, "Their anniversary. Ten, one, thirty-three." Mr. O'Malley nodded in agreement.

"All right, let's try it." Emma twisted the lock to the date Mrs. O'Malley had quoted. Her eyebrows shot up when a solid little *snick* was heard, and there was a sigh of pressure released as the door swung outward a tiny bit. Emma pulled the door open.

The interior of the safe was finally revealed. About

the size of the outside of the plaque that had covered it, it appeared both sturdy and deep. Emma held her breath as she leaned forward to see what might be contained in this safe that had been hidden in plain sight. The others crowded around as well, anxious to see the interior. A large jewelry box, cash, and a lot of papers filled the interior.

She pulled out the jewelry box and the cash. The others gathered around the desk as she placed the items on it. "I wondered why we didn't find much jewelry for Mrs. Kerwood," she murmured as she opened the lid of the jewelry box. She took in the glittering array of fine diamond earrings, bracelets, rings, and necklaces. Mrs. Kerwood had also had a penchant for sapphires, as there seemed to be more of those than other fine stones except for diamonds. There was nothing you would call ostentatious or brassy, but all in very good taste and expensive.

Emma picked up the cash. She was not in the habit of holding or counting large quantities of bills, but since the packages were in one hundred- and five-hundred-dollar packs, she guessed there were more than a hundred thousand dollars.

Mike pulled the papers from the back of the safe and laid them down beside the cash on the desk. As he rifled through them, he let his breath out slowly.

"*This...* " he said, "is what they were after."

Emma, the O'Malleys, and the police chief all moved to see what Mike had discovered. He placed the papers back down almost reverently.

"What are they?" Emma shrugged. She looked at the documents but didn't understand.

"Bearer bonds," the chief said. "And lots of them."

The stack looked to be about three inches thick.

"Bearer bonds," Emma repeated after him. "Those are bonds that are paid to whoever presents them, right?" She had, after all, learned a little bit in her time as a paralegal.

"That's right," Mike agreed. "You buy a bond and hold on to it, and it has interest paid on it. When you want, you can present it for payment on the principal and interest. There's a fortune in bearer bonds here."

Mrs. O'Malley looked at the items from the safe now spread across the desk. "You know," she said, "Mr. Kerwood always had this little spot of insecurity. He didn't talk about it often, but sometimes you got the feelin' he felt he might lose everything, and then where would he be? I'm thinkin' this was his security."

Mr. O'Malley nodded. "He was kinda funny that way."

"What I want to know," Emma put in, "is how the Karrolls knew about this safe and how to access it." She nodded toward the O'Malleys. "You lived with him a lot longer than Nancy Karroll. And you both said you didn't know of a safe in the house."

"No, we didn't," Mr. O'Malley answered. "But Ms. Karroll was with Mr. Kerwood at some of his sickest times, and she was prone to walk into a room without knockin' or invitation. It's possible Mr. Kerwood told her something when he was real sick, or she walked in here when he was using the safe and saw how he used it and what was in it." He nodded as he thought about it. "Yep, that's probably what happened."

"Okay, well, I've got to get back to the station," the chief said. "I want to personally oversee the processing of these two tonight." He looked at Mike and Emma.

"We'll need you both to come down and file a report, but it can wait until morning if you want."

Emma glanced at Mike and spoke for both of them. "I think morning would be a lot better, if that's all right."

"Sure. See you then." He put on his hat and left.

Emma looked at the O'Malleys and Mike and heaved a huge sigh of relief. She reached for the jewelry box that had been Mrs. Kerwood's. "Why don't we put all this back and go sit around the kitchen table? I think that apple pie is calling me."

Mike grinned and picked up the stack of bonds.

As the O'Malleys walked from the room, Mr. O'Malley said, "I'll make some coffee if you'll cut the pie." The older couple talked as they headed toward the kitchen.

Emma turned to Mike. "Do you think it's really over? Malone is gone and won't be back?"

"I won't feel completely out of the woods until I know Malone has been arrested," Mike answered. "I think the Karrolls were behind this, but I don't think they were the dangerous ones. I think Malone is the real threat."

"Mike." Emma stopped him. "It doesn't add up. Malone had me tied and no threat to him. He could have easily killed me but didn't. Why?"

Chapter Twenty-One

The next morning, Emma and Mike drove to the police station and were surprised to see the chief waiting for them.

"Don't you ever sleep?" Mike asked.

The chief grinned. "I wanted to be here to tell you the good news. Malone was apprehended at the Dallas airport. He'd bleached his hair, added a bushy blond mustache, and wore shoes with a lift to add height. A sharp police officer, aided by their security system, recognized him, and he's now behind bars where he belongs."

Mike shook his head. "To get away with so much over so many years, then to be tripped up by working with a couple of amateurs." He looked at the chief. "I assume the Karrolls are amateurs."

Grinning wider, the chief said, "Actually, they're not. This is the fifth plot they've hatched, all with similar scenarios. Nancy goes in as a nurse to an old rich geezer who's about to die. Long story short, between her and her brother, they manage to pretty well rob the old guy blind, then disappear right before or after he dies. In this case, her brother hired Malone to steal the brooch." He shook his head. "Mr. Sun wasn't supposed to get shot. Malone said he jumped him after he got the brooch."

Looking at Emma, the chief said, "Malone never wanted to kill you. That's not how he works. He is all about what's good for Malone. Toward the end, the Karrolls provided a good escape plan for him, and that's all he wanted. So, you were tied up and left to simmer but not killed."

He continued. "As to the Karrolls, I'm surprised Nancy didn't have the intelligence to know there would be a combination inside that lock that they'd have to use. From what we got from her, she saw Kerwood use it but didn't see that he had to have an additional combination to open it."

Emma sighed and looked first at the chief, then at Mike. "So it really *is* over?"

"It would appear that way," answered the chief. "If you two will just have a seat, we'll get your statements. I think both the Karrolls and Malone will be away for a good long time."

****

Filing their reports took the rest of the morning. Mike and Emma drove across the state line to Joplin for a leisurely lunch before they returned to the house.

Emma's eyebrows raised as they approached the house. Several cars were parked in the drive. "Tina's back already. My parents are here, too."

Mike opened the front door amid excited chatter from the living room. They hurried in to find Emma's parents and Tina on one couch, talking excitedly with Mr. and Mrs. O'Malley, who sat across from them on the opposite sofa. Mrs. O'Malley played the gracious hostess and set a refreshment tray on the coffee table. A few cookies were laid out for anyone with an appetite. Tina sat with a soft drink clutched in her hand.

"Well," Emma said, "Make yourselves at home."

They turned as a group. Emma's father stood to

greet them, then Emma's mother leaped and ran toward her daughter to give her a big hug. Emma winced in pain, and her mother stood back and gasped.

"Oh, honey, I'm sorry," she studied her daughter, noticing the purplish bruises. "Poor thing, you *are* rough-looking. Mrs. O'Malley told me about how you tore your bed apart after that awful man tied you up. Are you all right?"

"Yeah, Mom. I'm fine. Just a little sore." Emma gave her a quick hug back, not so tightly.

Kay Stone looked at Mike, standing quietly behind Emma. "You don't look as bruised as my daughter, but I understand you took a lump on the head. Are you okay?"

"Yes, ma'am," he answered, relieved when she didn't press any further. She might think he didn't do enough to protect her daughter.

"Come sit down," Emma's father called from the couch. "The O'Malleys have been filling us in on what happened last night." Emma, Mike, and Kay Stone all trekked back to sit and discuss the previous night.

****

Sunday afternoon waned. Emma's parents left to go to Broken Arrow after making tentative plans for a family Christmas party. Tina had gone to her room, and the O'Malleys had returned to their own house.

The bench at the front of the house had become a favorite spot for Emma and Mike to sit and talk. Marms dozed beside the couple. Mike's arm was around Emma's shoulders, and they leaned comfortably into each other.

"I know you haven't been here long," he started. "You've been busy getting settled in, the charity picking up stuff, and then this weekend, but have you given any thought about what you're going to do?" He waved his hand to indicate the house and surroundings.

"Not really," she answered. "I'm just gonna coast for a while."

He nodded, then abruptly stood. "I should get back." He looked uncomfortable, as if he needed to say something.

Emma rose and turned to face him. Her arms itched to reach up and curl around his neck, but she stood still and continued to watch his face.

"Is something wrong?" she asked.

"Maybe." He looked uncomfortable.

"Well?" Emma persisted. He remained silent and looked away from her, not meeting her eyes. Finally, she gave in to her impulse, lifted her arms to slide around his neck and forced him to look at her. When he did, she leaned in and pulled his face down to hers for a leisurely kiss. Mike's arms automatically wrapped around her.

As they broke apart, Emma continued to lean in, her head against his chest. "Is there still something wrong? It feels right to me."

He sighed as he rested his chin against the top of her head. "I've heard other officers talk about how emotions run high, and they get involved with someone from a case they're working. It's not the real thing, but they're in too deep, and someone or everyone gets hurt." His voice cracked.

Emma twisted out of his arms to look at him. "So, you think that's what this is? The case has caused us to be emotional and drawn together?"

He was unable to look her in the eye. "Maybe."

"What do you want to do about it?"

"I would like to see you again. And again." His

smile was a bit shaky. "How about *we* just coast along for a while, too?"

She nodded. "I'm willing to go along with that. When's your next day off?"

Epilogue
Six months later

The Grand Lake Stone Lion Inn had been in business for three months, and Emma had never been happier. She sat on the front bench as a cool summer breeze ruffled her hair. Emma wanted to take a break, while Marms desired a nap across her lap. He'd slink across her legs and sprawl. She'd gently pick him up or push him away. Then the scene repeated.

Lifting her arms in a leisurely stretch, she mentally reviewed the last few months. Going back to school had been a scary decision but the right one. Emma had excelled in hotel management, and the city of Grove had been more than happy to re-zone her property for an old-worldly bed-and-breakfast inn that proved to be a tourist magnet. Two majestic stone lions had been added to the entrance of the property at the highway, thus completing the name *The Grand Lake Stone Lion Inn.*

She had a skill in keeping customers content, and it made her happy to see them smile. So far, she could only recall one couple who seemed determined to be cranky despite what she offered.

In her element, Mrs. O'Malley fixed breakfast and a light lunch for the guests and her choice of desserts and snacks. Emma employed another woman from the local area to help on her days off. She'd also procured a couple of reliable young women for the housekeeping duties.

Similarly content, Mr. O'Malley remained as

groundskeeper, doing what he loved to do.

Emma stood and stretched again, further dislodging Marms. He looked up at her and squinted his eyes. A car approached and drew his attention. He perked up at the sound of that engine.

Emma didn't recognize the sound of the engine, but the man she'd grown to think of as *hers* was behind the wheel. When he'd parked and exited, she trotted down the steps to meet him, arms wide for a welcoming hug, which he quickly obliged.

"I've got news," Mike announced after he kissed her. "I'm excited, and I hope you will be, too."

"What is it?" Anxious to hear, Emma let Mike take her hand and lead her back to the seat.

He rubbed Marms's head as he sat down and tugged Emma down beside him. Mike took a deep breath. "I want to open my own private detective agency in the Grand Lake area. The police chief has offered consulting on the side to help with their cases, even some cold cases." Hope shone in his eyes. "We could see each other more often."

Emma frowned slightly, confused. "But what about your career with the Tulsa police? I thought you loved being a detective."

"It's not the Tulsa position I love. It's the work I do that I love."

Emma continued to look doubtful, so he explained further. "I love solving crimes. Helping people get closure when their loved ones have been hurt or murdered, and they don't know who killed them or why. Even the crimes that aren't that serious, breaking and entering, drug cases, catching the bad guys."

"Where will you live?"

"Somewhere in Grove." He looked serious and took her hands. "I just want to *be* here, with you, instead of two hours away all the time."

Convinced, Emma laughed and swung her arms around him, giving him a long hug followed by a lengthy kiss.

Marms jumped down and looked at them. His eyes squinted, and he moved away to sit and study his people.

"I hoped you'd be happy about it." Mike let out a long breath and put his hands on her shoulders, gently guiding her to sit down on the bench to face him. He kneeled in front of her.

Emma's eyes grew, and she sucked in her breath.

From his pocket, he pulled out a slim, silver diamond engagement ring. "It's not much," he said, "but I wish you'd wear this and agree to marry me."

Emma's eyes were round and glued to the ring. The diamond was small, but that didn't matter. She blinked, tears threatened, and her mouth trembled as she spoke. Lifting her left hand, she whispered, "Yes, yes, yes!"

He slipped the ring on her finger, and they stood up together.

Cupping her face in his hands, he kissed her gently.

When she spoke, her voice cracked. "It was my lucky day that you got assigned my case, or I never would have met you."

"No." He shook his head and smiled. "It was *mine.*"

A word about the author…

Joy M Ross has lived in Oklahoma over twenty five years. Raised in Missouri, she still adheres to the "Show Me philosophy" when something sounds doubtful. Her roots are now planted in Broken Arrow, where she gardens, reads, writes cozy mystery novels, and scary short stories. She travels when possible as learning the ways and traditions of others are always interesting.

An animal lover, she has two troublesome terriers, a tuxedo cat, and most recently, a large chocolate lab. All rescues, and all placed in her life by God.

joymross.com